scrooge-ish

A FLIRTY, OVER-FORTY, SILVER FOX, SECOND CHANCE HOLIDAY ROMANCE.

L.B. DUNBAR

www.lbdunbar.com

Cover Design: Megan Dunbar
Editor: Emerald Edits/Nicole McCurdy
Editor: Gemma Brocato
Proofreader: Karen Fischer

Other Books by L.B. Dunbar

<u>Sterling Falls</u>
Sterling Heat
Sterling Brick
Sterling Streak
Sterling Clay
Sterling Fight
Sterling Touch
Sterling Stone

<u>Chicago Anchors</u>
Elevator Pitch
Catch the Kiss

<u>*Parentmoon*</u>

<u>Holiday Hotties (Christmas novellas)</u>
Scrooge-ish
Naughty-ish
Grouch-ish
Elf-ish

<u>Road Trips & Romance</u>
Hauling Ashe
Merging Wright
Rhode Trip

<u>Lakeside Cottage</u>
Living at 40
Loving at 40
Learning at 40
Letting Go at 40

<u>Silver Foxes of Blue Ridge</u>
Silver Brewer
Silver Player
Silver Mayor
Silver Biker

L.B. DUNBAR

<u>Sexy Silver Fox Collection</u>
After Care
Midlife Crisis
Restored Dreams
Second Chance
Wine&Dine

<u>Collision novellas</u>
Collide
Caught

<u>*The Sex Education of M.E.*</u>

<u>The Heart Collection</u>
Speak from the Heart
Read with your Heart
Look with your Heart
Fight from the Heart
View with your Heart

A Heart Collection Spin-off
<u>*The Heart Remembers*</u>

BOOKS IN OTHER AUTHOR WORLDS
<u>Smartypants Romance (an imprint of Penny Reid)</u>
Love in Due Time
Love in Deed
Love in a Pickle

<u>The World of True North (an imprint of Sarina Bowen)</u>
Cowboy
Studfinder

dedication

To all the grinch-ish ladies out there during the holidays,
I see you. I feel you. I relate to you.

the reunion

chapter 1

I hate Christmas.

I don't know who thought every female must love shopping, wrapping, baking and hosting—as commercialized on nearly every holiday advertisement—but if those things are supposed to be coded into my DNA, I'm missing it.

And my hatred is exacerbated each year by gifts given more from obligation than love, well wishes without heart behind them, and family.

Don't get me wrong. I know Christmas isn't about gifts. The season wasn't born in a store, and I believe that kindness can be found in a word or smile just as much as a deed, but something is always missing for me.

Somewhere along the way, I stopped caring about this holiday.

Maybe it was when certain people stopped caring about me.

Refer back to reference three above: Family.

What's the worst is I work in retail, where the happiest time of the year is accentuated by the beep-beep of chip scanners, the screaming emotional meltdown of children, and annoying, selfish customers. I'm in management at Ashford's, a top-end department store in downtown Chicago, open seven days a week because my boss is an asshole.

I work a lot of hours, volunteering to fill in for others because they have families, or family emergencies, or friends with families who have emergencies, and more work for me means more money toward my dream. It also means less time facing reality.

I don't have a life.

And I'm lonely.

But no worries. It's late Wednesday, Thanksgiving Eve, which has somehow become a thing on the night before an American holiday, and I'm working.

"What are you still doing here?" Zaleya asks me as I hand over two bulging bags of random clothes to some older woman who has no idea what she's just purchased for her grandchildren. Cha-ching, cha-ching, though…

"I'm working."

"But you were off at six and now it's eight." Zaleya Stone is a curvy brunette with a huge heart and an infectious smile. She's excellent with difficult customers and a dream to work with.

"Eight. Six. They both have a little, swirly circle at the bottom of them." I shrug giving Zaleya a smile. The Ashford's smile. The I'm-happy-to-work-here-even-though-I'm-really-miserable-but-need-the-money smile.

"Ev-a," Zaleya draws out my name. At least she says it correctly. Ev-ah, like Evan without an -n. Not Eve-ah, or even Evie, or Eve, or whatever name Jude Ashford likes to say when he grows frustrated in a management meeting and can't remember my name despite eight years working here and making top manager three years in a row. Jude is younger than me and the owner of the entire company. He's also hot which makes him even more annoying, but I'm not into the cougar-thing.

"You have a thing tonight," Zaleya reminds me although I really don't want the reminder. I mean, who celebrates twenty-two years since high school graduation? We were supposed to have a twentieth in 2020, when a world pandemic hit, and the celebration had to be cancelled. Then the alumni organization wanted to host a glorious twenty-one the following year, only the planning committee members contracted COVID from each other. Gossip on the street, though, is the cancellation was because a set of former high school sweethearts and two former jocks leading the planning had a four-way one weekend that ended a marriage and a business partnership. It was a scandalous situation the high school couldn't allow affiliated with the reputation and prestige of good old Immaculate Academy.

"Oh, I'm not going." I force another smile as I nod at the next customer to step forward. I shouldn't be working a register, but the floor is busy despite being the night before Thanksgiving. We're running a door-buster deal this evening as a jumpstart on Black Friday's five a.m. opening time. We used to open late night on Thanksgiving, but we've canceled that extra evening of potential revenue. To be closed on a national holiday actually felt rather compassionate which wasn't my thing.

I've been told I'm selfish and unfeeling, according to my last three attempts at relationships. And while I tend to agree with that assessment, I stopped caring a long time ago.

"You have to go," Zaleya admonishes me.

"I don't have to do anything." I ring up a female customer's purchase, hoping she isn't intending to wear the two items purchased in combination.

Zaleya nudges me out of the way before the next customer steps forward, swipes her team member card through the register, and logs me off the system. Somehow, she's overridden the program and clocks me out of work.

"I could write you up for insubordination and unethical practices." I narrow my eyes at her, without any heat in my threat. Zaleya is older than me by almost two decades, but under me as an assistant manager.

"One day that veneer is going to slip, and you'll realize a real softy lives beneath that tight leather skirt and take no prisoners heels." Zaleya winks.

"Don't you mean others will realize . . . and also, you're wrong. Nothing soft here." I pat my belly, which actually does jiggle a little and grumbles, reminding me I haven't eaten all day.

"Yeah, well, eat some peppermint bark or a Christmas cookie . . . or five. And put some roast beast on those bones." She eyes me up and down, and I marvel at her use of a Grinch reference.

I like Zaleya. She reminds me of the mother I never had, which doesn't make sense as my mother is still around. Can't have a memory of someone who didn't exist, though. Mom left on Christmas Eve, when I was ten, and Dad cancelled the holiday that year. And most years after that. Zaleya is more like a mentor, or a guardian angel, if I believed in such a thing. She's just an overall nice person, and I hate her a little for her good cheer. But not really.

Zaleya nudges me out of the register station. "Get going. I predict great things from this evening."

+ + +

By eight-thirty, Zaleya catches me still lingering in my meager office on the upper floors of Ashford's. The flagship store is the last remaining Ashford's. The company was bought out, and all but the landmark location was converted to the other conglomerate's brand. Gossip around the water cooler, so to speak, is that Jude inherited the single store, instead of the brand going to his father. As the sole family member who owns Ashford's, I've heard words like spoiled, entitled, and ungrateful for his inheritance used to reference him. On a side note, we don't have water coolers because Jude is too cheap to pay for such a service for his employees.

"Eva." Zaleya's motherly tone is both admonishing and chagrin.

"It's too late to go."

"It's only eight-thirty. You young things are just getting started at this hour."

I'm no longer young. I'll be turning forty this December.

"I'm not dressed."

Zaleya eyes my outfit, taking in the leather pencil skirt in bright red I'm wearing. I'd worn it in an effort to appear holiday-cheery when I'm not.

"You look gorgeous."

"I'm too old to attend these things. I mean, who goes to high school reunions, really? Jocks who can't let go of state championships two decades-old and still wear their high school rings. Nerds who want to show everyone they made it financially. The pimply kid who wants to prove he was a supermodel underneath his skin. The homecoming queen who popped out three kids before thirty and is divorced from her second husband."

Zaleya stares at me.

"Where does that put me?" Not jock. Not geek. Just your average girl in high school. Good grades, clean-cut, and boring.

"It puts you attending. Not to prove anything to them but to allow yourself a night out on the town among people you once knew."

"But that's my point. I don't know these people anymore. I hardly knew them twenty-two years ago."

"Just go. 'Tis the season." Zaleya waves a hand above her head. "Magic is in the air."

"The season doesn't officially begin until tomorrow, when Santa drives his sleigh before Ashford's in the parade." Sarcasm fills my voice. I don't believe in Santa any more than I believe in magic.

Zaleya puts her hands on her hips. "Honey, Christmas lives all the year through."

Jiminy Cricket, she sounds like a holiday card.

"Who knows? Maybe an old boyfriend will be there." Zaleya wiggles her brows.

I snort.

"Or a boy of former interest." Her voice hitches, gushing with innuendo.

I huff.

But someone does come to mind.

Someone I deny myself the chance to remember, as I'm certain he's forgotten me.

+ + +

O'Malley's isn't exactly out on the town. The slender pub lined by a bar on one side and tight, upright booths opposite the counter has had two additions over the years. A second bar is attached to the first room, and a seating area outdoors in a side yard is the third space. O'Malley himself was a sponsor of Immaculate Academy, as an alumna, and he loved hosting these casual, impromptu reunions. The pub is one of those corner locations tucked in a Chicago neighborhood and known for its loyalty to the University of Notre Dame. On any given weekend, the place is packed with Fighting Irish supporters. A mixture of Christmas lights and gaudy tinsel springs hang among the ND paraphernalia of signed jerseys, Irish sayings, and shamrock cutouts in all shapes and sizes.

After entering the pub, I elbow my way to the bar.

One drink and then I'm out of here.

Leaning on the countertop, I'm trying to get the bartender's attention, but she keeps ignoring me. I'll count to four before I give up on ordering. Suddenly, someone bumps into my back, elbowing me hard between the shoulder blades and I pitch forward against the bar. I'm wedged between two people on high top stools and a man turns to face me as I lean forward. Of course, he knocks over his mostly full beer, and I spring back, hoping to avoid a waterfall of hops pouring down on me.

This causes me to elbow whoever is too close behind me.

"Whoa, darlin'," a thick masculine voice says behind me, and a hand comes to my lower back as I watch beer cascade over the bar and puddle at my feet.

"Sorry," I mumble as I twist to face the person.

Then I'm tongue tied.

Zebb?

Before me stands Zebb Scroggs. Scholarship kid. Top athlete. Excellent student. And my high school crush that turned into a secret summer affair before we both went off to college.

I'd always wondered what happened to him. Not that it mattered. We had our summer and went our separate ways, but still . . .

"Eva?" Dark delicious brown eyes meet mine and sparkle like hot chocolate under the twinkle of the Christmas lights suspended over the bar. His mouth hangs open, moist from drink and surrounded by a light brown scruff speckled with white. Snow on damp sand best describes it. Laugh lines crinkle on the corner of his eyes and the eventual smile on his lips causes my heart to race in a forgotten way. The way only he caused it to patter.

"Zebb," I shout over the noise of the crowded bar. Glancing to the side, the spillage from the beer continues to cascade to the floor. There isn't much space between the sticky bar and Zebb's body, but instantly, I'm tugged against his solid chest when a possessive arm wraps around me.

"What the hell?" Zebb chuckles and addresses the man on the stool. "Brock."

Brock has righted his fallen glass but didn't bother to mop up the spillage. With unfocused eyes, he stares at me.

"Do I know you?" Brock asks.

"Don't hit on my girl," Zebb admonishes.

What the heck?

"You shouldn't even be here," Zebb adds.

"I'm here for the freshmen," he slurs.

"You mean fresh meat and you're too old for this crowd. You graduated three years before us."

My mind swirls as I swivel my head from this Brock to Zebb. Then it clicks. Brock is Zebb's older brother.

Zebb watches the last of the beer spill over the lip of the bar. "This place is a mess tonight," he shouts. "And so are you." He scolds his brother as his arm around me tightens.

"Come here often?" I yell again, despite our proximity, which is me plastered into his side with a hand against his firm chest. His flannel shirt is soft. He smells of campfire and whiskey, and his heart pumps beneath my palm.

"Are you trying to pick me up with that line?" He laughs, deep and rich but quiet like I remember. A sultry chuckle, like his laughter is a gift and the sound a limited edition. A secret even. He used to laugh with me, though.

"What? No." His flirtatious comment has me flustered. I wouldn't know how to pick up a man any better than the Grinch could properly steal Christmas.

"Okay, sexy Santa's helper." He smiles, one side of his mouth curling higher than another. "Was that your drink that spilled? Let me buy you another."

"Now who sounds like they're casting out pickup lines."

"I'm definitely casting." He winks at me, still holding me at his side. Realizing I've been hanging onto him for longer than is probably appropriate, I press on his chest to move away from him, but his arm around my lower back tightens in response.

"Hey AJ, we need a rag here. Help Brock get an Uber and give me two shots of Fireball."

He definitely comes here often if he's familiar with the bartender, and I snort into his soft flannel, inhaling him once more before my brain registers what he ordered.

"I can't do shots."

"Why not? It's cinnamon-y goodness. Perfect for the season."

Groaning, I try again to pull away from him. He smells too good and that voice of his . . . it got me in so much trouble that summer.

"I hate this season," I admit, loud and proud over the noise.

His head snaps downward, those yummy chocolaty eyes narrowing. "What kind of Scrooge are you?"

"A realistic one."

Zebb smirks, continuing his perusal of my body molded against his. "A beautiful one." While his voice softens, his words are loud enough to be heard.

"Are you drunk?" I laugh, anxious that he'll say yes. That his arm around me should be a warning instead of a reminder of his touch when we were young. A reminder of his hold on my heart back then.

"Nope." He pops the *P* and I'm still not convinced.

A towel has been placed over the spill of beer and the bartender swipes it up before placing two shots on the countertop.

Still clutching me, Zebb hands me one glass then reaches out for the second one.

"What should we drink to?" he yells over the crowd. We're collectively jostled in this tight space between bar stools and a crowd of standing people.

"I don't know," I admit, more worried that I'll be wearing the Fireball instead of drinking it.

"To reunions, then." Zebb taps the lip of my shot glass with the side of his and tosses back the cinnamon-y goodness in one smooth move. I watch his Adam's apple roll along his throat and my mouth waters for a taste of his skin just below the sharp edge of his trimmed scruff.

Sweet baby Jesus, does he look good.

He turns those hot chocolate eyes on me, and I hesitantly lift my glass to my lips. The scent hits my nose before the spicy liquid cascades over my tongue. My throat burns from the sharp alcohol, and I sputter and cough, not nearly half as graceful as him chugging down a shot.

Zebb pats my back as I set the glass on the bar top. The movement releases me from his side and a shiver runs up my body from the absence of his warmth. When his hand settles on my nape, beneath my hair, he leans near my ear.

"Let's step out back where we don't have to shout."

I nod, giving into the heat of his hand on my neck and the gentle guidance he gives as we make our way through the crowd until we reach an exit to the side yard. A canvas tent has been set up to cover another bar, and tall outdoor heaters warm the rectangular space which isn't more than sixteen by twenty.

"So," Zebb says once I'm leaning against the wrought iron fence lining the yard. "Eva Nazar." He eyes me again. I'd unzipped my long jacket upon entering the bar and my coat hangs open, exposing my red skirt and knee-high boots. With thick, knee-high socks peeking out my boots, I'm dressed for protection against the cold more than fashion.

"Zebb Scroggs," I state, taking in his flannel shirt, buttoned up but hinting at a dark t-shirt beneath it. He's wearing dark pants and black work boots.

"What have you been up to?"

His question reminds me that this right here is why I didn't want to attend this shindig. I don't do small talk. I chatter all day, attempting to be cheerful with strangers who pass through Ashford's. The last thing I want to do is recount twenty-two years in a few sentences with a man I used to know.

"We don't need to do this," I blurt, lifting my eyes to meet his. He's over six feet and almost a foot taller than me even as he leans over me with a hand above my head, clutching the fence behind me.

"Do what?" His smile grows again. He was incredibly good looking as a teenager. Aging agrees with him. Those eyes. That grin. The addition of facial hair.

"It's been a long time, Zebb."

"And it was too short a summer." His words cause my gaze to lock with his.

Zebb was the kind of boy you dreamed about but didn't experience in your reality. He came from the southside of town, and everyone knew he was at Immaculate Academy on scholarship. He wasn't judged for it, but the status gave him an edge. A hint of untouchable. Mystic even. He's the kid you went to high school to watch but would never enter his circle. Then one night at a party near the end of senior year, he cornered me in a manner similar to our current position. Arm over my head. Fingers touching my hair. His eyes full of mirth and mischief.

And he kissed me.

The shot of fireball should have been a reminder.

Zebb tasted like cinnamon gum and something sharp, something warm and dangerously close to all I'd ever wanted when I was young.

"Okay. Let's get the basics out of the way." He breaks the silence that has lingered too long between us. "I majored in finance, but realized money isn't everything."

"Really?" I exaggerate the adverb. Money was my sole purpose. To make it. To save it.

"Now I'm a firefighter."

"A firefighter?" The mental image of Zebb in a CFD uniform has my girly parts slowly smoking. Then again, he'd always looked good in his football uniform.

He doesn't mention that between his finance major and being a fireman, he was in the NFL. This is the only thing I know about him.

"Your turn." His fingers coast along the part in my hair, like a movie scene from some teenage film. Girl against locker. Guy leaning over her. That never happened to me in real life.

"I'm a manager for Ashford's."

"The department store?" His brows lift.

"The one and only." My gaze lowers to our feet for some reason. His large boots are on either side of my slender heeled ones. I should be cold standing outside, but Zebb is like a personal space heater, crowding me in and warming me up.

"I thought you were in Colorado." His voice lowers, full of confusion and questions.

Leaving had been my plan. I went to college in Colorado, thinking it was so trendy to head for the mountains and get away from a major metropolis. Only, I wasn't a ski-loving weed-smoking kind of gal (though there was nothing wrong with either thing). I'd missed the familiar. I transferred schools and came home. Then I floundered for years before landing at Ashford's.

Somehow, admitting all that makes me feel like a failure, so I don't explain myself.

"Now I'm back."

His eyes narrow. "How long?"

"How long what?"

"How long have you been here."

"Almost twenty years."

Zebb hisses under his breath and presses off the fence. He stands taller and slips his hands into his pockets. His frame is so much larger than I remember. His shoulders are wider. His legs thicker.

"You've been here all this time." His gaze drops to our feet. His voice quiet as if I wasn't meant to hear him. Then his head pops up. "I thought you wanted to open a bookstore in a small town."

Or a soap shop or a specialty boutique, but that was neither here nor there.

"Oh, well, that dream died." Dismissively, I wave, brushing away the lie. The dream still lives deep inside me, but the reality is too far away to envision. I'd gone to school for business management. I wanted to be an entrepreneur of sorts. Working in a department store had not been my end goal but when I returned to Chicago, the only job I could find at first were salesclerk positions.

I briefly explain how I worked my way up through Ashford's management program and tell Zebb my current accolades.

"Impressive." With his brows lifted, the spark in his eyes says he means it. A sly smile curls his lips. "How is your dad?"

"He moved to South Carolina."

As an eighteen-year-old daughter, and an only child to a single father, I had freedoms I suspect most young girls didn't have. It was easy to sneak out of my house or sneak Zebb in which was a huge advantage in keeping our summer fling a secret. I wasn't ashamed to be seen with him. If anything, he didn't want people to know we were together.

Want to keep you all to myself. My foolish young heart believed the sentiment.

After I went to college, I lumped Zebb in with my mom and dad. I just wasn't good enough for anyone to want me long term.

"He had a heart attack." Yep, shortly after I returned to Chicago, my dad decided to move away and my last shred of familiar was gone.

"Oh, I'm sorry to hear that."

The next hour passes in the small talk I dread but I learn more about Zebb. His mother, brother, and sister still live in the area. His nephew goes to Immaculate Academy, not on scholarship.

The reminder hints how different we'd been as teenagers. I'd never been to his home. He hadn't introduced me to his family. We didn't do public things.

The way he kissed me then made none of it matter.

But there's still one topic he hasn't mentioned.

"And you made it into the NFL."

Until Zebb, Immaculate Academy had never had someone play for a national-level football team. I didn't follow sports much. I only knew he'd made it big. He'd gone where he wanted to go. He'd taken the

Tennessee Wildcats to the Super Bowl two years in a row. He'd lived his dream.

Back when we were kids, we didn't talk much about the future, but we shared our desires. He wanted fame and fortune. I wanted a simple life, moving to a small town, and owning my own business. I also wanted a real family, but an eighteen-year-old girl doesn't tell her summer fling such a thing.

Turning his head, Zebb squints off to the side. "It wasn't meant to last forever. I've been back for a while as well."

The city was so vast it wasn't shocking I hadn't run into him over the years. We wouldn't have traveled in the same circles anyway. I didn't have a circle. I had Ashford's.

When Zebb doesn't offer details to his return, silence falls between us. There are only so many sentences that encapsulate two decades of history and exhaustion hits me as well as the cold. I've rezipped my jacket and tucked my hands into my pockets, but an endless chill ripples over my skin.

"I think I better cut out." I nod at the dwindling collection of people outside. I haven't spoken to another person the entire time although people have passed Zebb, patting him on the shoulder, offering him a handshake. He still has a charismatic persona, drawing people to him like a magnet. Surprisingly, his attention always returned back to me standing beside him.

"Don't go yet." Zebb has moved closer to me, leaning his side against the fence. His chest has been pressing against my arm.

"I have to work."

"Not tomorrow," he chuckles.

Thanksgiving is another holiday I don't celebrate, but I don't mention it.

Instead, I softly smile at him. *No, tomorrow I have other plans.* "It was great seeing you, Zebb."

He pouts but presses off the side of the fence. "How did you get here?"

"I Uber-ed."

"I'll walk you out, then." He wraps his arm through mine and tugs my hand from my pockets. "Where are your mittens? Your fingers are freezing."

I laugh at his fatherly voice. "It's cold outside." I don't know how he hasn't noticed while wearing only a flannel shirt.

"All the more reason to stay," he singsongs and wiggles his brows.

"Is this about to turn into a Christmas song?"

His expression shifts. "You know that song is not what people have made it out to be. It's a classic. He really did want her to stay."

"But he spiked her drink."

"Maybe it was only Fireball." He winks at me.

Shaking my head, I agree with him but express my forward-thinking thoughts. "Everyone brings their own experiences to that song."

Like I have experiences with Christmas as the reason I loathe the most wonderful time of the year. *Insert sarcasm.*

With Zebb holding my hand, we easily walk through the less crowded rooms and stand outside on the curb. I've pulled up the Uber app and ordered a ride.

"Well, *my* experience is I really want you to stay." He rubs his thick thumb over my knuckles. Lifting my hand, he wraps both his palms around mine and blows on my cold skin in the cavern he's made. Another shiver ripples over me but it has nothing to do with the temperature.

"And I really must go," I sing back to him and then we both laugh.

"I remember your laugh." The corner of his mouth quirks up.

"I remember yours." Suddenly, I'm filled with melancholy as we speak of an action that represents joy and a long-ago history between us. We stare at one another, but I can't read his eyes like I did when I was eighteen. When I recognized a look before he kissed me. Or the awe before he slid into me.

How strange it is to encounter someone who once had carnal knowledge of your body. Knew where to touch you and how to please you, and you learned the same things about him.

Time and distance changes everything. Our experience now is two strangers.

A dark sedan pulls up beside the curb. "This is my car."

"Eva…" His fingers clench around mine, holding me in place as I try to take a step away from him. Our eyes meet again.

"Yes?" Our arms are outstretched. Me leaning toward the car. Him standing on the curb. Fingers still clutching at one another.

He tugs me to him, and I inhale his scent once more. Cinnamon and firewood. His scruffy cheek brushes against mine and his breath tickles my ear. "It was great to see you again."

Then he releases my hand and steps away from me.

And that's where this reunion ends.

chapter 2

Thanksgiving passes as a reflective day. I don't celebrate with family but spend the afternoon serving food at a homeless shelter. This doesn't make me a good person. I'm only here once a year, but as I don't have plans for a big meal, this is how I've spent the past decade.

Afterwards, I visit my mother. Yes, the woman who left when I was a child has recently resurfaced in my life.

As always, visiting my mother leaves me feeling disjointed. I tell her about Zebb, the reunion, and work. I'd often felt I'd like to reach out for her hand, maybe hold it while I speak, but we didn't have that kind of relationship. Even calling her mom is a struggle. After fifteen minutes of one-sided conversation, I excuse myself and leave.

When I return home, I call my dad. He asks about my mother. The question is terse, and I imagine him clenching his teeth. My father is bitter about her return. Still bitter from her initial leaving. But he doesn't have a say in my seeing her. *He* doesn't have to see her. He's in South Carolina with his new woman, a later-in-life romance involving two people who met on a golf course. It's sickeningly sweet and gag-worthy uncomfortable to know my father has more sex in his sixties than me nearing forty.

"If you don't want to know, why do you ask?" My haughty question doesn't soften him.

"I want to support you. Her return must be difficult." He hasn't really supported me since he left this city. He gifted me the down payment on my one-bedroom apartment in the West Loop out of guilt.

In many ways, his leaving was harder. I'd come back to Chicago, and he turned around and left within three months. The symmetry to Zebb is remarkable. Zebb left me after high school. My father left when I transferred colleges. I'm never certain which departure hurt more.

Then again, my father hadn't been actively involved in my life any more than my absentee mother. I'd been alone for a very long time.

"I'm fine," I lie regarding my mother's return. Then I end our call.

The weight of the day presses down on me. My thoughts have repeatedly returned to Zebb.

When we were kids, he'd climb the fire escape late at night and we'd fill the time with us in bed, exploring one another, learning one another, being together. Since seeing him last night, a montage of what we had runs through my head. Of what I wanted us to be.

Foolish teenage dreams.

+ + +

The next morning is a rush with an early alarm and harried customers. I don't work a register as much as wander the floors, all seven of them, checking on clerks, supplies of register tape, and sales per department. The store looks like Whoville moved in for the winter. Boxes and bows, ribbons and taffeta. Gold and silver plus red and green colors every surface. Millions of mini bulbs twinkle and Christmas carols ring out on every floor. Garlands are strung wherever they can be hung, and Christmas trees fill every crook and corner.

When Ashford's lost their worldwide reach and took back their original philosophy, an overhaul was made as to what they carried and how merchandise was displayed. I'd been to the famous Liberty London which carries high end house goods, some personal effects, and fancy fabrics. Ashford's leaned in that direction upon their revival. Shopping here was intended to be an experience. Dining. A theatre. And floors of furniture, housewares, fashion, and personal items. Jude Ashford's great-great-grandfather would be proud of his great-great-grandson's vision in the modern age, although the original owner might grimace at his descendant's arrogant attitude.

He has just bitched me out for a child puking in the children's department. I've called maintenance and I'm taking a much-needed break in my small office when a knock comes to my door.

"Special delivery." Zaleya sails into my office holding a vibrant red poinsettia plant.

"If that's my Christmas bonus, I don't want it." Last year, in an effort to cut back, Jude gave his top management a gift card to McDonald's, another Chicago-based business. I'd thought the card was a joke at first, but Jude claimed he was supporting other big businesses with a show of comradery. Three of our managers quit the day after Christmas. Jude didn't understand he was a large *small* business and he needed to act as such.

"Actually, it was hand delivered. When I overheard the hunk of a man asking where he could find you, I offered to bring this up."

A personal card the size of a greeting card was attached.

Zaleya set the plant on the corner of my desk and held out the envelope. I flipped it open and pulled out a card stock sheet of people.

What did the Grinch say to the Who?

Turning over the paper, the back read: *My heart grew three times its size at the sight of you.*

My face heats.

"Girl, your cheeks are the color of this flower. What does it say? And who sent it?"

I swallow around the strange lump in my throat and glance back at the plant. "His name is Zebb." My voice isn't more than a whisper as I stare at the pointed leaves. "We went to high school together."

"And you saw him the other night?" Zaleya's voice rises in hope.

"We talked."

"Old flame? Spark rekindled?" she teases.

I stroke a finger down the silky red petals, luxuriating in the feel of it while shaking my head. "He wasn't a boyfriend." He'd been so much more in a sense. A secret lover. A new experience. I'd given my virginity to him. "Did you know a poinsettia is a funeral plant in Mexico? It's a sign," I say, pulling back my fingers from the vibrant flower.

"We don't live in Mexico. And a sign of what?" Skepticism fills Zaleya's round face.

"Death."

"Eva!" Her hands fist at her sides as her eyes widen.

"Or a sign to leave the past where it should be. Buried behind me." I pause, staring at the festive holiday bloom one more second before looking at my co-worker. "What's that saying about rearview mirrors? No sense looking backward." I place the card back in the envelope and lay it on my desk.

"Honey, what I wouldn't give for one more night with my Harold." Zaleya had been married thirty-six years when her husband passed away. She speaks of him fondly but has moved on in her own way. "Girl, where are your daydreams and wannabes?"

I had them. I just didn't share. I couldn't think about it yet. I had a ten-year plan, and I was only at year seven.

"Wishes are for fools," I whisper. The statement isn't intended to hurt her but a comment on my own hopes.

"Eva, while most people want to forget their pasts, and that's probably a good thing, the past can also hold some of the best memories. Moments in time we carry with us as a reminder that we lived, we loved. We hurt." She clasps her hands together and clutches them to her chest. "There's no shame in remembering as long as it doesn't harden your heart. We learn from the past. We know things from it. Good things." Her voice softens as her expression shifts. "You can shut the door on some things, but you need to open a window and let in the fresh air. The pleasant memories. The ones that molded you into the person you are."

I huff. Only bad things molded me. My mother disappearing. Then reappearing. My father leaving after I returned. Failed relationships. A forgotten business plan.

"Eva." My name brings me out of my thoughts. "That fresh breath of air is waiting in the makeup department."

"What?" I blink, uncertain I understand.

"Zebb, you said his name is? He's downstairs."

+ + +

I didn't exactly run from my office, but I did briskly walk to the elevator bank and jab the down button more times than necessary. I smoothed my hand over my emerald-green wrap dress, another nod to the season, and straightened my name tag. When the doors finally open, I rush inside and turn to face the mirrored wall, double checking my hair. I should have applied more lipstick.

Then I stop myself.

I didn't need to primp for Zebb. I had no idea why he'd send flowers to me. Why he'd *deliver* the plant himself and write a personal card. But it didn't mean anything.

Tis the season, he'd said the other night. People were overly generous this time of year.

As I finally arrive on the first floor, I realize I hadn't asked Zaleya which makeup counter. Several more minutes pass as I wander around the maze of holiday decorations and display cases, some areas more congested than others. I've gone from one corner to the next and don't see a man in a flannel shirt looking like a youngish Santa. Then I turn to a man dressed in a navy blue, short-sleeve button up uniform shirt, signifying he's a fireman. He's admiring something in one of the cases as I approach.

"I'm not certain pink is your color."

His head pops up and his gaze scans my body. "Green is certainly one of yours." His teeth pin the corner of his bottom lip a second as he looks up at me.

"Do you know how impossible it is to get a manager in this place?" His hot-chocolate eyes sparkle even in the bright florescent light of the store.

I slowly smile. "Thank you for the flower." We stare at one another as we did the other night. It's hard to believe he's standing in Ashford's. How many times has he been in the store, and I've walked right past him? Or has he been in here with a girlfriend, a wife even, and ignored me?

Then again, he was surprised to learn I worked here.

"Are you shopping for your girlfriend?" I nod at the makeup case. Stepping over to it, I slide my hands along the edge. "Or your wife maybe?"

I won't be the other woman in either case.

"Eva." He leans against the display, crossing his arms. He stands close to me, and heat radiates off his body. "Topics we didn't cover the other night. No girlfriend. No wife. And you?"

I twist and glance up at him over my shoulder. "No girlfriend. No wife either."

He chuckles. "Boyfriend or husband then."

"Neither of them as well." Our eyes lock once more.

"So what are you doing here?"

"Delivering a plant to a pretty girl."

"Girl?" I scoff.

His eyes rake down my body again. "Gorgeous woman."

Fighting a grin, I chew at my lower lip. "Interesting selection for a flower."

"Do you have something against poinsettias?" He tilts his head. "I was trying to be original." He glances over my shoulder.

"Ahh…" His voice softens and I turn to see what he's looking at. Behind me is a huge arrangement of poinsettias. The entire first floor is filled with strategically placed traditional holiday plants.

I turn back to him while his eyes remain over my head another second. "It was the thought that counts, though, right?" *He really is sweet.*

He looks down at me. "I'll do better next time."

"Zebb." There doesn't need to be a next time. I'm still not certain what he's doing here this time.

"Give me your number." The way he demands instead of asks instantly throws me back in time to the night we first kissed. He dared me as we stood in the backyard of that party. I'd never been the first to advance but he stood perfectly still as I stepped up to him. I only intended to brush my lips over his, but he caught my upper back before I pulled away and kissed me back. Harder. Deeper. The next thing I knew I was making out with Zebb Scroggs. He demanded that night I give him my digits.

From that moment on, "Toxic" by Britney Spears was my theme song. Zebb was poison for my heart, but I couldn't get enough of him.

"Zebb, we don't need to do this."

"Do what?" His eyes held mine.

We don't need to relive the past. We don't need to reconnect in the present. There is no future for us.

"I just want to call you sometime." Slowly, his lips curl.

A man approaches us from the side, and I turn as another fireman pats Zebb on the shoulder. "Ready, chief?"

"Almost. I'll meet you outside."

The other man eyes me up and down. "This her?" He tips up his chin assessing me. He isn't a bad looking man himself, but he isn't all-consuming like Zebb.

"This is her." A smile fills Zebb's voice, and I turn back to him wondering what that smile means or what this man knows about me.

The fireman thumps twice on his chest, gives us the peace sign with his fingers and steps away.

"So, number?" Zebb pulls out his phone and I recite my phone number while it feels like Santa's reindeer are taking flight inside my stomach.

What are we doing?

My own phone beeps inside my pocket and I pull it out.

"You can label that too-hot-to-handle, if you'd like."

I laugh. I don't recall him being so openly cocky. "And what are you going to label me?"

"Well, when I told the guys I needed to stop here, I labeled you a five-alarm smoker. But now it has to be poinsettia potential."

I wrinkle my nose, not liking the name. He holds up his phone and snaps a quick picture.

"Hey. That's not legal without my permission."

"As I recall, we once did lots of illegal things without permission." His eyes skim up my body again and my skin heats.

I'm certain red washes my skin and lights me up like a Christmas beacon in my green dress.

Without a final farewell, he turns to walk away like he did the other night.

Once he disappears through the exit I remember where I am—work. I brush back my hair, straighten my shoulders and spin in the direction of the elevator. I don't make it to the bank before my phone rings. I quickly check the number and answer.

"Hello?" A giggle fills my tone.

"I said I wanted to call you sometime and I figured now is as good a time as any."

Silence fills the line as I step aside to let others take the lift. I'll lose the phone connection in the elevator, and I'm not ready to sever whatever this is between us.

"Go to the game with me this weekend."

"What game?"

"Immaculate Academy is in the state finals. The game is tomorrow night."

"Oh, I have to—"

"Don't say work." I hear his smile through the phone as his voice deepens.

Slowly, I wander toward one of the store's entrances, seeking privacy. "Zebb, really, I have to—"

"My nephew is playing. He's the quarterback, remember? I really think they'll win."

"Zebb, work—"

"I get it. Work is important to you. Is that always going to be your excuse? Not washing your hair. Or having other plans. Just work?"

Was work my excuse for not doing things? I do have a plan. I need to work. Work was my life.

The thought hits me hard.

I didn't have a life.

As if tired of waiting for an answer, Zebb remarks, "I used to be like that. Thinking work was all I needed. But work can cost more than the money it earns, babe. Think about it."

A pause fills the line. His *babe* wasn't derogative. It wasn't sweet either. He's probably called plenty of women babe over the years.

"Listen Santa's helper, the man in red can spare you for an evening. Come to the game with me."

I chew my lip and glance out the expanse of glass doors leading outside. A fire engine turns the corner.

"Did you drive a fire truck to the store?"

"Had a special delivery to make."

My breath hitches and that team of reindeer in my belly swirls around once again. "Okay."

"Okay you'll go?"

"Yes. I'll go with you, Zebb." I'd said something similar to him the first time he showed up at my place. He'd climbed the fire escape up three floors and knocked on my bedroom window. I had no idea how he knew it was my room, but my thoughts were filled more with the surprise of finding the boy who kissed me like I was the air he needed to breathe crouching outside my window.

"I'll text you the details. Til tomorrow then."

"Til tomorrow."

chapter 3

Zebb arrives for our date in a pickup truck. The ride to the state championship will take roughly two hours as it's held at a central university. The night is cold, and I've bundled up as best I can. However, the inside of his truck is warm and toasty and within minutes, I'm peeling off my jacket.

"No red or green tonight."

I glance down at my clothing. I'd pulled out an old hoodie with my graduating year on the back which dates me. The item is the only thing I had with school colors on it. I hadn't attended many athletic events during my high school years. If Zebb had been my boyfriend, I wouldn't have missed any football games.

"Went with team spirit tonight."

"You're team spirit alright," he teases, while weaving onto to the highway.

"What does that mean?"

"Each time I've seen you, you look like a sexy Christmas greeting card."

"I do not." I snort-laugh and Zebb swivels his head to look at me. His mouth falls open at the sound and I cover mine with two hands. He chuckles before biting the corner of his lip, holding the tender skin pinned under his teeth for a second.

"You must love the holiday."

"Actually, I hate it."

He sharply turns to me and then, just as fast, back to face the windshield. "How can you hate Christmas? What Grinch spit in your hot chocolate?"

"My mother," I quickly retort before considering what I'd said. Silence falls between us. "You might remember I didn't have a mom growing up."

Zebb nods. "And you might remember I didn't have a dad." His absence is one reason Zebb had a scholarship to IA.

Zebb stays silent and the quiet calls for me to explain. I don't typically share this story, but we have two hours to fill.

"She left on Christmas Eve when I was ten." I wasn't ready to explain why she decided to go or how she had returned.

"Fuck." Zebb's knuckles whiten where he grips the steering wheel.

"Yeah. My father canceled Christmas that year. And most years after that."

"I'm so sorry, Eva."

I shrug. "No worries."

He glances at me once more. "But that shit messes with your head. And your heart." The softening of his tone hints he understands.

I don't respond.

"Well, we need to make you new memories for Christmas then. Get you back some holiday cheer." His voice rises.

"I think I'm a little beyond believing in Santa Claus."

He gasps. "Don't say such a thing or he won't visit you."

"Oh my God." I laugh. "He isn't real."

"Ah! You just crushed my hopes of a new Tonka truck."

I glance around the interior of what looks like a relatively new pickup. "I think you'll be alright."

"Okay, seriously. What did you want for Christmas when you were ten?"

"Zebb." I groan and tip my head against the back of the seat. "I don't even remember."

"Try to think of something."

"I don't know maybe a Barbie Golden Dream Camper RV or a Doll and Me doll."

"Baby doll or look-alike?"

My head pops up from the seat and I turn to look at him. "Look-alike, I guess."

"Golden Dream Camper RV is pretty specific. Why that toy?"

I gaze out the front window. "I wanted to escape reality, I guess." My parents were always fighting. I shouldn't have been surprised my mother left. Her sudden disappearance from my life was more the issue.

"Have you ever been camping?"

I huff. "No."

"Don't say it like it's beneath you?" He glances over at me, laying his wrist over the steering wheel.

"I'm not. I've just never been camping." I hesitate. "We vacationed every Christmas until I went to college but nowhere that pushed the holiday. Tropical places where Christmas didn't make sense."

Zebb's brow pinches.

"I've never been to Disneyland either." I shrug again. "It's not a big deal."

"Robbery." He's teasing but the joke hurts. I wouldn't say my childhood was stolen. My father did the best he could raising a girl on his own, but he also wasn't overly involved or loving either.

"So tell me more about this nephew of yours."

"Nick is my brother's son." Pride fills his voice. "Brock was the asshole who spilled his beer on you the other night." Zebb rolls his eyes.

"He'll be here tonight, of course. He also has a daughter, Eleanor."

"Do you miss it?" I hesitate. "Football."

Zebb cautiously smiles. "Yes and no." He pauses. "One of my first words was ball. I got a football when I was about eleven, and the second that ball was in my hands I knew it was my future. It's all I wanted to do. But things happen. Plans change."

"What happened with the NFL?"

He squints through the windshield at the dark sky. "I told you. Some things are more important than money."

"But what about the game?" I push.

Zebb seems to contemplate something before saying, "Still love the game but now I'm a spectator."

There's something he isn't telling me. He'd been at the height of his career when he suddenly wasn't playing anymore.

"The truth is we aren't all Tom Brady. We can't play much past thirty. I'd been sacked a few too many times. Ankle injury. Wrist issues. Tweaked my back once. I was getting old."

I laugh, though not to hurt his feelings. "Well, you look good for an old guy."

His head turns again, and his eyes sparkle in the glow off the dash. "You think I'm good looking?"

"Oh, come on. You know you are." Suddenly, my hands sweat. What am I doing with this man again? He's so different than me. Successful. Confident. Gorgeous.

"You're even more beautiful than when we were teens." His voice is soft.

My face heats. He's good at this. "Wow. That was sweet."

Memories return. How he'd kiss me slow and tender. How he took his time discovering the places I needed him to discover. How he triple-checked that I wanted to give my virginity to him.

"I never wanted to hurt you."

"I know." I whisper, suddenly missing that girl who wanted a boy so badly she could hardly sleep some nights. And remembering a girl who missed a boy when that summer ended.

"Why did we break up again?" The question is playful while his tone is curious.

"Summer ended, I guess."

"Yeah, summer ended."

This isn't a topic I want to discuss. How hard it was to walk away from him. He had dreams. I had goals. He was going to make it big, and he wouldn't have wanted some girl hanging onto a summer fling like it meant something. We weren't in love. At least, he didn't feel that way about me. And I never would have exposed my feelings to him. He wanted to get away from Chicago just as I did but for different reasons. His future awaited him. I wanted to leave my past behind.

After a few minutes of silence, I reach for the radio and turn up the volume. We shift to safer topics like music we love and current movies we've seen.

The past goes back into its box, wrapped in permanent paper, and sealed with a bow.

+ + +

I haven't been to a high school football game since . . . high school. But it wasn't lost on me that some things never change. The students still had sections within their section. The band kids. The rambunctious senior boys. The quiet girls up and to the back filled with unrequited love for one of those rowdy teens.

The family section didn't feel much different, collecting people by cliques. This neighborhood. That subdivision. This Catholic parish. That suburb of Chicago.

Zebb leads us through people who want to shake his hand, acting as if they were long lost friends. Comments about his former status are given. Those who know his nephew as the current star quarterback offer congratulations although the game hasn't even started.

Eventually, Zebb guides us up the bleachers, higher than most of the crowd, and to a bench with two women sitting side by side.

"We thought this might be better for you." While one woman speaks to Zebb, the second woman does a double take at me. She has similar features as Zebb—light brown hair bordering on a rusty red with deep dark eyes—and I recognize her as his younger sister, Marnie.

"Thanks. Where is Brock?" Zebb references their older brother.

"He's down there pacing the fence by the sideline." The woman beside Marnie explains. Her voice is rich and face beautiful with coal-black eyes and long lashes. Her lipstick is a deep plum color, and her dark hair is swept up in a plethora of braids.

"Jesus. He needs to cut Nick some slack," Zebb grumbles.

Both women huff to agree.

"Marnie. Lisa. This is Eva." The way I am presented makes me sound like a specialty dish. Our main course tonight is . . . Eva. And for dessert, we have . . . Eva.

"Hi." I wave weakly as Zebb spreads out a sleeping bag, providing us a cushion on the cold, metal bench.

"Eva?" Marnie was a freshman when we were seniors. She can't possibly remember me, but her gaze zings from me to Zebb. She stares at her brother, who ignores her prying eyes.

"We can pull this up and around us if we get cold," he says to me.

I smile as I take a seat. The air temperature is around thirty, and I dressed accordingly. Long underwear underneath lined leggings plus knee-high rider boots and my insulated thigh-length winter jacket. I wear a beanie cap and scarf but seem to have forgotten gloves. Sitting still, it doesn't take long before I'm chilly. While Zebb seems to be comfortable in only a flannel shirt and tee, tonight he wears a heavier jacket and a beanie cap as well.

"I'll get the awkward out of the way." Lisa leans over Marnie and Zebb groans on the other side of me. "How long have you two been dating?"

"Lisa," Zebb moans and lightly laughs.

"Babe," Marnie grunts.

"I'm only asking what we both want to know." Lisa peers up at Marnie while leaning over her lap and the look they share makes it clear they are a couple. "He never brings a woman to these things."

"Oh my God." Marnie giggles and turns to me. Her cheeks are pink and her eyes sparkle. "I'm so sorry about her."

"Eva went to Immaculate with me," Zebb explains. "We ran into each other at O'Malley's the other night. During that reunion."

The reunion where I didn't reunite with anyone other than him.

"Ah," Lisa hums before sitting upright on the other side of Marnie.

"Coffee? Hot chocolate?" Zebb asks me.

"I'd love a coffee," Lisa blurts.

"He wasn't asking you." Marnie laughs again.

"Well, as long as he's going. Coffee. Yes, cream and sugar. You know how I like it, handsome." Lisa winks at me as I watch her give her order.

"Ignore her," Marnie mutters. "I'll take a coffee as well."

"I'd love a hot chocolate." It's probably going to be watery with all the chocolate lumped at the bottom, but something warm does sound good.

"I can't carry four drinks," Zebb states, glancing back at Lisa.

"Fine. I'll come with you."

Marnie's mouth falls open as Lisa stands. Facing one another, Lisa looks down at Marnie. "Get all the deets while I'm gone." She slides by me and meets Zebb on the stairs.

He shakes his head and points at his sister. "Behave."

Marnie grumbles. "I'm always good."

We watch as the two clamber down the metal steps.

"She wasn't wrong. Zebb never brings anyone to these games." Marnie's voice is soft, defending her woman while offering some truth about her brother.

"I'm not certain if this is an accusation, like I'm intruding on something sacred, or I should feel honored." I laugh to dispel the anxiety.

Marnie shifts, facing me with doe-like eyes, wide and worried. "Oh gosh. That wasn't an insult. We're just . . . surprised. Zebb talked about you all through Thanksgiving."

"He did?" I sound like an eager teenager but the tension in my shoulders lessens. "It's been a while since we've seen each other. This isn't really my scene." I point toward the field.

"Well, this is Zebb's church, so get ready to worship football for two hours." Marnie laughs again, the sound light and easy. "I'm a teacher, so I understand athletics can mean a lot to some people. Zebb always had focus. Brock is just a madman." She points at her eldest brother who is still pacing the fence near the sideline. "Zebb will need to rein Brock in and bring him up here or he'll torture Nick. He's one of *those* dads."

"Those dads?" I wasn't an athlete in high school or ever, so I don't know what she means.

"The kind who scream and yell, commentating on the coaching, cussing out their own kid or other players on the sideline. More than once Zebb told Brock if he didn't knock it off, he'd physically remove him. Our nephew is grateful." Marnie softly smiles and glances down at her lap. "Brock is just jealous of the life Zebb once had, you know. He lives vicariously through Nick and wants him to follow in Zebb's footsteps."

"That's a lot of pressure on a kid."

"We know. That is Zebb and I know. Zebb felt like he had to do well for our family. He wanted to provide for everyone when it wasn't his responsibility."

My gaze shifts to the concession stand where Zebb waits in line, people leaning in to chat with him.

"Everywhere he goes people want to relive his glory days, but he'll say his best life is now." Marnie shakes her head, glancing in the same direction as me.

I'm still processing all these snippets as to who Zebb is now when Marnie changes the subject. "So what do you do?"

I spend a few minutes explaining my job. The strange part is, I don't feel like I'm on an interview or filling space with small talk. Marnie seems truly interested and I imagine she makes a great friend.

"How long have you and Lisa been together?"

Marnie removes her mitten-covered hand and holds it up to me. A gold band circles her left ring finger. "We were married last year. We've been together for five." Love beams from her face as she stares at the symbol of her commitment to another person.

"Congratulations."

"Thanks." Marnie turns to me while replacing her mitten. "I've never been so happy."

She practically glows and a twinge of envy pinches me. I'm not an artist but the expression on her face could immortalize happiness. Like moonbeams and sunrays and rainbows might pop out of her.

I don't think I've ever looked that way about anything. Or anyone.

Zebb and Lisa return with our collection of drinks and the pre-game announcements begin. Zebb excuses himself one more time to gather his brother and bring him up to our seats.

"I wasn't saying anything to him," Brock grumbles as they reach our bench. In the bright lights of a football stadium, I have a better view of Brock than I'd had at O'Malley's. He's broader than Zebb, though they're the same height. His hair is covered by a baseball cap and the hair on his face is more stubble than scruff, as if he shaved this morning but it's already growing back.

"Just sit down by Lisa and try to keep it together." Zebb points to the other side of Lisa.

"Why do I have to babysit the beast?" She narrows her eyes at Zebb.

"Because I brought a date."

My head swivels to look at him while his brother chortles.

"What a putz. You don't bring a date to a high school football game." The bench quakes as Brock tosses his larger body onto the seat beside Lisa and swipes his baseball cap off his head.

"And what do you know about dating?" Lisa chides Brock.

"I know plenty. And you don't bring a woman to a high school game."

"You don't know nothing," Lisa digs. "That's why you're still single as a Pringle."

"I'm single because my ex-wife—"

"Just shut your kisser, mister," Lisa scolds.

"Jesus. Maybe this was a bad idea," Zebb mutters as he lowers beside me.

Without thinking, I reach out for his thigh. "This will be fun." And I'm surprised I mean it. Watching him interact with his family is entertaining. As an only child, siblings are always a wonder to me.

My hand slowly slips from Zebb's firm leg, but he captures it before I can fully retreat. "No gloves, again?" He chuckles.

Then he tugs my fingers higher up his thigh and covers my hand with his. "This reminds me of high school."

"You played football in high school," I jeer. He never sat in the stands.

He looks at me over his shoulder and lowers his voice. "Maybe this is one of my fantasies then." His gaze holds on mine.

A whistle blows and the game begins. We sip our drinks. Yep, my hot chocolate is warm water with chocolate somewhere at the bottom of the Styrofoam, so I set the cup beneath the bench, out of feet range.

"You don't like the drink?"

I wrinkle my nose. "I'm all good."

Zebb sighs. "I really am a cheap date."

"Isn't that supposed to be my line?"

Zebb looks at me before swiping at hair dangling out from beneath my knit cap. "Nothing about you is cheap."

There's a compliment in there somewhere and I softly smile.

The game plays and Zebb switches his left hand over mine for his right to keep my hand pressed to his upper thigh. His arm wraps around me and he tugs me into his side. I shiver against him.

"Cold?"

"Only a little."

Quickly, he maneuvers the sleeping bag up and over our shoulders. The material is double wide but covers more of me than him.

"Aren't you cold?"

"I have all the warmth I need." He tightens his arm around me which is tucked under the cover of the thicker material.

We sit like this for only a few minutes, Zebb calling out when a play goes well, or grumbling when a fumble happens. My dad loved football and watching it was something we did together when I was younger. That doesn't mean I understand the game. Still, the enthusiasm for the sport ripples off Zebb and his family members, and I settle into his side, laughing at their antics.

"Scramble to the left, Nick."

"Catch it, damn it."

"Aw. What was that call?"

The chatter is its own soundtrack.

Zebb's hand slips from over mine and slides over my thigh. Gently, he squeezes while his arm around my back tugs me tighter to him.

The game continues but I can't seem to concentrate on anything other than Zebb's fingers kneading my upper leg and dipping between my thighs. His fingers stretch and clench. He isn't near the promised-land, but he's close, working me up with just a simple squeeze and a constant tease against my leg.

A rhythm beats between my thighs, matching the occasional thump of the band's percussion section.

I tighten my hold on his thicker thigh. He'd brought my palm higher up his leg. If I were to stretch my fingers, I'd brush against something I probably shouldn't be thinking about touching as I sit in the stands of a high school football game.

"Are you enjoying the game?" Zebb's question is low at my ear. His breath tickles the tiny bit of skin exposed. I turn my head and find his face close to mine. He kneads my inner thigh, pressing tighter, slipping slightly higher. My legs involuntarily spread an inch, allowing him space to climb, providing him a hint to reach deeper.

That beat between my legs grows to a constant rumble, like a droning drum.

I swallow around an answer to his question. *Was I enjoying myself? We shouldn't be doing this.* He shouldn't be touching me like this with his sister on the other side of me. She can't see anything with the blanket over my shoulder and legs but still . . .

"I'd always wondered what it would be like to be a spectator."

"You never attended football games?" My voice is weak and labored as he clutches my leg and hitches it over his thigh. My hand is pinned in his lap as he brings my body even closer to him.

He leans into my neck and whispers near my ear again. "Never like this."

I gaze back at the field. My concentration on the game is completely lost. Zebb continues to massage my thigh, and my hand pinned near the zipper of his jeans feels something firm and growing beneath the snug denim. I squirm the slightest which brushes my fingers against him, and he stills.

Something happens on the field. Zebb comments as if nothing is happening on this bench.

"Come on. Get in there. Defense."

I lower my lids as his voice ripples outward, but his pinky finger slides upward and swipes at my center. With my leg hitched over his, I'm opened up beneath the sleeping bag.

When I don't move, his entire hand slips closer to the apex of my legs, and more fingers ripple over my core. Despite the layers of lined leggings and long underwear, heat emits from my center. Wetness dampens the seam.

This is so wrong.

I squeeze at the sudden bulge in his jeans, long and hard, jutting against the space where his leg meets his lower abs.

Memories of our past flood me. The first time I touched him. The first time I put my mouth around his firm length. The first time he entered me.

My breath shortens.

Zebb straightens his back. He moves his hand up the inside of my leg, bringing the outside of my knee against the back of my hand over his stiff cock.

"Behave," he mutters through clenched teeth while hardly moving his lips.

"Me?" I choke. He's the one working me up beneath a thick blanket with his sister beside me and a stadium full of football fans.

I glance at the score clock to see we only have a few minutes left in the half.

The players line up for another kickoff. They pat their padded legs, and the student section matches the beat by thumping their feet up and down on the metal bleachers.

And the rumble matches the growing pulse in my lower lips.

Zebb only pauses his attention on my leg for a second before his hand skims down my inner thigh again as the kicker races for the ball.

He kicks and the crowd cheers. Zebb doesn't stop his momentum. Direct and firm, he cups me and my hips rock before I register what I'm doing. What he's doing. Where this is going to lead.

"Who needs the bathroom?" I quickly stand and toss my portion of the sleeping bag over Zebb's lap. My question is breathless like I'm the one chasing after the receiver who caught the ball.

"There's only a few more minutes before half-time," Lisa says.

"I'm going to beat the rush." I slide past Zebb's knees, and he grabs my hips as I work around him.

"I'll go with you," he says, standing quickly behind me and lifting the sleeping bag, holding it before his waist.

"That might not be the only thing she beats," Brock mutters.

"Dude," Zebb hisses, but I'm already skipping down the steps, willing my body to calm down. The sudden wash of cold night air helps. My eyes prickle with frustration. I'd been on the verge of an orgasm. One I shouldn't be having in such a public way with a man I hardly know now.

I weave my way toward the bathroom as my name is called from somewhere behind me. Once inside the restroom, I lean against the wall, waiting out my turn and wishing away the disappointment.

Why was Zebb touching me that way?

Once I do my business, wash my hands and take a quick glance at myself in the mirror, I exit the bathroom to find Zebb waiting.

"I'm sorry," he mutters, chagrin on his face. He rolls his lips inward and then twists them side to side. "Let's take a break."

He cups my nape and leads me as he did that night in O'Malley's.

"Where are we going?"

"To the truck. We can warm up during half-time."

Doesn't he mean cool down? My insides are on fire while my skin registers the cold.

"Do you really think that's a good idea?" I question as he guides me to the gate where we have our hands stamped for re-entry.

He's quiet a second, before saying, "I promise *I'll* behave."

Once we near his truck, he opens the driver's door and helps me up. His truck is parked in one of those dark spaces between overhead lights, and due to the crowd, we're quite a distance from the stadium. I slide over allowing him space to enter. He presses the ignition button and fiddles with the temperature gauges. A blast of cold air hits us before he turns the fan down and presses the seat warmers on.

"I fucked up, didn't I?" He tugs his knit cap off his head and tosses it beside him.

"No," I whisper. "I just . . ." *Was on the edge of an orgasm.*

He turns his head to face me. "Fuck. I just want to kiss you."

I swallow against the eagerness of a response and choke out, "Okay."

His eyes widen before he cups the back of my neck and tugs me forward. We meet in the middle where his forehead gently presses to mine before he dips in with his lips.

The kiss is soft at first. A sip. A swipe. Nothing like I remember.

Then he opens, firm and desperate. His kiss is like flipping the switch to light a Christmas tree. The mini-lights flicker on, and that first glance brings a gasp and then awe, and you realize something so beautiful means so much more than presents beneath it. That's the feeling growing inside me as his lips move over mine.

He takes control of my mouth like a master-kisser, guiding me to follow his lead. Our lips press together then spread, savoring one another before his tongue sneaks forward and mine meets his. That touch sets off a frenzy where I'm pressing my upper body closer to his and his hands lower to my backside, tugging me to him. We kiss harsh and hurried as I slip my arms around his neck and his palm spreads on my lower back.

"Are you warm enough to take off your jacket?" He mutters against my mouth while reaching up for my hat. My hair crackles from the cold reacting to the heat of the truck's cab. I quickly unzip my coat and shrug out of it as he pulls my scarf loose and unwraps the material.

We rush in for another desperate kiss as I cup his jaw in my hands. The prickle of his scruff is like a live current down my body and I arch into him again. He struggles with his own jacket, popping snaps and releasing the zipper, while trying to remain attached to me. I press at the outerwear, helping him remove it.

"You taste exactly as I remember."

I smile, ready to respond but his mouth is back on mine. His hands squeeze my back and pull me closer to him.

"Damn this hoodie." He chuckles, referencing my bulky sweatshirt, as he moves from my lips to my jaw, gently scraping his teeth against it.

"I wore it for warmth," I explain of the old spiritwear that hangs long enough to cover my backside.

"I want to warm you." He returns to my mouth, his kiss fast and frustrated. His fingers delve into my hair and tug my head back, tipping it so he can suck at my chin and lick underneath it. "Let me worship you."

Holy Christmas. *Who says that?*

"How?" I choke before he returns to my mouth for another fierce kiss.

He pulls back. "Sit on my lap. Face the steering wheel." He presses a lever on the side of his seat and the entire chair moves back providing more space between the wheel and his body.

"I'm wearing a ton of layers." Frustration fills my tone but it's too cold to remove everything despite the heat of the truck and the fogging windows.

"I'll figure it out." He guides me up and over him, which is an awkward climb of moving legs and bumping into the steering wheel before I'm facing the windshield with my back to his chest.

"Did you like what I was doing to you on the bleachers?"

"Aren't most kids supposed to make out beneath them?" I tease.

His hands curl around my waist and slip under my sweater to discover another layer of clothing. He quickly tugs it upward, scrunching it up until he can get his hands on my skin.

"I would have spread you out on that bench and taken you right there if there weren't thousands of people in the stands."

"Not to mention the frigid temperature," I stutter as the heat of his palm seeps into my flesh.

"Mmm." His nose traces the lobe of my ear and I twist my head toward him. "Eyes forward. Hands on the wheel."

"Why do I feel like I'm in driver's ed?"

"Did you ever want to fuck the instructor?"

"No," I choke out.

"Then this isn't driver's ed." He pauses as he fumbles with my waistband, slipping his hand beneath the tight restriction. "Slip your legs to the outside of mine."

I do as he says, straddling his lap as my knees hit the outside of his.

"I could still give you a driving lesson, though." He hums at my ear as his palm spans my lower belly and I tip my head back to his shoulder.

"First rule is no reversing. There's no going back once I touch you again."

I have no idea what he means but I close my eyes and nod.

"Next, I could park right here if that's all you want." He cups his palm over my underwear like he did in the stands, only the heat of his hand meets dampness. "Jesus, Eva. You're soaked."

Tell me something I don't know.

"With your permission, I'd like to drive through this lesson."

I huff. "Your puns are almost dad-worthy."

He hums at my ear again. "Answer the question. Red light or green?"

"Green. Definitely green." My hands clutch the steering wheel, knuckles turning white with the tension to hold on as Zebb slips a finger beneath my underwear and swipes through sensitive folds eager for the ride he's about to give me. I rock into his touch, which forces my backside against the bulge in his pants. He pauses to adjust himself and the pressure of his cock slips between the crease of my ass.

"Eva," he groans in warning and want. A second finger dips into me and I hunch forward a second, clutching the steering wheel as he fills me. My legs spread wider but are restricted by my pants.

"Wish you were wearing that red skirt right about now. Or maybe the gorgeous green dress."

I exhale as his fingers draw to the edge and then quickly rush forward again.

"Christmas apparel." I have no idea why I say that.

"You could wear an ugly Christmas sweater and I'd still find you beautiful."

"Zebb," I cry out as the precipice he drew me near while sitting in the bleachers quickly rebuilds. I rock over his lap, rolling my hips. I'm gripping the steering wheel before me so hard, my fingers ache.

"That's it, my little Christmas queen. I'm going to make you come."

"You know I hate this holiday." I'm gasping as I attempt to reprimand him.

"I'm going to change your mind. One orgasm at a time."

Baby Jesus in a manger. What is Zebb doing to me?

I don't consider his words as truth, but enlightenment is dawning on me. I tighten around his fingers and thrust against his touch, and brightness fills the back of my lids as I come like I've never come before.

My head tips back to his shoulder and my back arches, forcing my hips upward and his fingers deeper.

Angels sing. Stars sparkle. A Christmas miracle occurs in the cab of this truck.

Slowly, I settle back down and Zebb pulls his hands from my pants. I lean forward, resting my forehead against the steering wheel, breathing hard, until I heard him mumble around something.

"Tastes just like I remember."

I roll my head to see him sucking on his fingers. Only the movement reminds me of the thick wedge straining his jeans and poking my ass. I wiggle against him.

"Eva."

I straighten and return my gaze to the fog covered windshield.

"One more driving lesson." I giggle as I move, pressing my backside at that firm ridge.

His hands land on my hips, squeezing hard. "You'll make me come in my pants like a randy teen."

I purr this time, working my hips back and forth until he takes the lead, forcing me to rub up and back over him.

"I can't believe I'm doing this," he mutters behind me. His head lowers to my shoulder a moment before he tips back and drops his head to the back of the seat. "What are you doing to me?"

I softly smile to myself as I continue to move, dragging myself back and forth over him, reminding me of how he felt beneath me, how he fit inside me.

Suddenly, I stop squirming and he curses. With awkward movements, I wrangle my legs back together and struggle to spin. My knee hits the steering wheel and then my backside beeps the horn. We both laugh before I'm facing him, straddling him.

"New riding lesson," I mutter before my mouth meets his and I press against him. My clit hits just right against the firmness of his shaft and I'm quick to rock up and back once more. His hands return to my hips, and he guides me as he heavily exhales. He glances down at us. Me in his lap. Him surging upward.

We both seem trapped in the memory of what it once felt like to have him inside me.

"God, I fucking want to fuck you." His words are harsh but soft, almost a prayer of need, and they bring me quickly back to the precipice.

"You might . . . I think . . . this never happens." I'm lost in my head as my body takes over and rubs against him like I can erase layers of fabric and drive him into my body. "Zebb?" I'm suddenly questioning everything. His name. My purpose. The meaning of the season.

"That's it, Eva. Again." His fingers press at my hips, rocking me faster over him.

My breath hitches. I gasp and then I'm spiraling out of control again like the red stripe swirling around a peppermint stick. I wrap my arms around his neck, and he thrusts upward once, twice, three times before he stills. Exhaling heavily near his ear, I hear him grunt and a jolt against my sensitive folds tells me he let go.

My forehead presses to his right shoulder while his head leans against mine.

"Was that a lesson in handling a stick shift?" I whisper.

Zebb begins to chuckle against my shoulder. Then he throws his head back and lets out a good laugh, one jostling the both of us as I remain in his lap. He leans forward for a quick kiss and then pats my backside.

"I might have some napkins in my glove box."

I take his meaning and shift off him, wincing at the stretch of my thighs. I open his glove compartment and pull out a wad of thin paper napkins.

He tugs his shirt upward and I glance away allowing him some privacy. He softly laughs. "Don't think this is going to make a bit of difference." He tucks the used napkins beneath the seat, and I face him.

His eyes spark in the dim light within the truck.

"Why do I feel eighteen again?" He's staring at me when he asks.

I shrug. "I don't know. But I'd never want to go back." The words immediately feel like the wrong thing to say. I don't mean anything against him. It's just if I went back to eighteen, I'd only lose him all over again. "That didn't come out right."

He softly harrumphs and tips up his chin watching me another second before looking at the fogged-over windshield. His hand dangles over the steering wheel and he swipes a finger over the condensation.

"Should we get back to the game?"

Why do I feel like I've just kicked Rudolph?

"Think half-time is over?" I reach for my hat and tug it back over my head.

"The third quarter is probably finished."

My mouth falls open. "What will they think we were doing?"

He rolls his head and then tilts it.

"Oh my God. This is so embarrassing."

"Still embarrassed to be seen with me?" He falls back against the seat and reaches for his cap.

"What? No. Why would I ever be embarrassed to be seen with you?" I sigh. "You were the one who didn't want to be seen with me."

He slips his hat on his head and peers over at me. "That was never the case, Eva." He huffs. "You didn't let me take you out."

Is he serious? "You never asked me out."

"I did."

"You did not."

He climbed my fire escape like my own personal Romeo. Or maybe Tony coming for Maria. And I opened the window and let him in. We didn't go out. My bed was our restaurant. My shower a movie theatre. We touched. We had sex. But we didn't date.

We stare at one another, in a stalemate, and then we both laugh at how we sound which lessens the tension a little bit.

"So will you go out with me again?"

My brows pinch as I look at him.

"There's a holiday party next weekend. Be my date. It's a costume party. It'll be fun."

Go out with him again? Was tonight really a date? He'd said such a thing to his brother and sister, but I didn't think he was serious. We were only old friends attending a high school football game together. Then again, what we just did says more than friends. Maybe it was just another reunion. A reminder of how good we were together. A reminiscence of what we had.

Why do I feel eighteen again?

I had no idea. I didn't know how he felt about me back then. He liked me, sure. We had fun discovering one another. But was it more than a summer fling before college?

I doubt it. At least for him.

"I don't know what I'd wear." I tug on my winter jacket and fix my scarf around my neck.

Zebb snaps up his jacket. "You'll have a whole week to figure something out. Say yes."

Was I really doing this?

"Okay," I whisper, chewing my lip.

A new question arises.

Why does going on a second date with Zebb feel more like a second chance with him?

the party

chapter 4

He'd called me angel.

After our late return to the game, Zebb had us stand near the sideline fence instead of returning to our seats. I stood in front of him, and he wrapped his arms around me to keep me warm. When Immaculate Academy won, we hung around until Zebb could congratulate his nephew. On the two-hour ride home, I'd fallen asleep leaning on his arm.

"You're home, angel," he'd said to me.

I blinked awake, dazed and confused. I'd been having this dream where he hadn't left that summer. Or at least we hadn't lost touch and I'd been beside him through his NFL career. Not that I wanted the fame or fortune, but just to stand by his side.

Or maybe I wanted him by mine.

When the following Saturday arrives, I have a costume although I'm nervous. He'd given me the idea without knowing it. The item had been in the back of my closet for years and I wasn't even certain it would still fit. I couldn't remember if it was from college or my twenties, but I hadn't been able to part with the costume for some reason.

"You're an angel." The corner of his mouth crooks up in a smile and his gaze is warm and direct when I open my door. I live in a one-bedroom condo. A large island separates the galley kitchen from the living space. The layout is pretty simplistic.

"I'm an angel," I confirm, tugging at the side of the flowy white dress. Then I spin so he can take in my wings. The wiring within them was a little bent but I was able to re-shape most of the kinks. The outfit looks strangely like the angel in the 1988 movie *Scrooged*.

"And who are you?" Before me stands a handsome man wearing a dark green robe with thick fake fur up the front and around the collar. A rope belt is tied around his waist while he wears a wreath on his head.

"I'm the Ghost of Christmas Present."

Slowly, his costume makes sense as well as feeling prophetic. I can't believe I'm going to a work party with him. Wasn't this something someone did after dating for years, not as a second date?

Zebb does a quick eyeball sweep of my place and smiles at the bouquet of red tulips in a vase beside my reading chair. Sunday morning the arrangement arrived with a green ribbon around the stems. He'd double checked the meaning of tulips after I told him about poinsettias. A new card was attached.

Tulips because my two lips want yours.

He was so cheesy.

"You look beautiful." Zebb holds out his hand. "Ready?"

I can't wear a jacket with my wings, but I do grab a clutch that holds my phone and house keys. Holding his hand, we step into the hallway.

"When you called me angel after the football game, I remembered I had this costume in the back of my closet."

He leads me to the staircase and then waves for me to take the lead since my wings take up space.

"I called you an angel because you looked like one sleeping on my shoulder."

I smile as the sentiment is sweet.

"But maybe you're really the Angel of Christmas Past."

I laugh as I reach the exit door and press it outward. "More like a ghost from the past."

Zebb takes my hand again and leads me to his truck parked at the curb. "Not a ghost. But definitely someone who has haunted me all these years."

I pause as he opens the passenger door. "Haunted you?"

He leans on the door while swiping loose hairs around my ear. I'd put my hair up in a messy twist and left shorter pieces loose here and there.

"I've never been able to forget you."

"Did you want to forget me?" Suddenly my throat is thick with the possibility.

"No. Not ever."

I chew my lower lip before stepping closer to him. "I never forgot you either." Tipping up on my toes, I kiss him, quick and soft. When I pull back, he catches me with a hand on my upper back and draws me back to him for a longer kiss.

"Maybe you're an angel of what's to come."

"And what's to come?" Or who. Pick your interrogatives.

"A second date." His playful tone brushes off anything more serious. "Would it be strange to say I missed you this week?"

I shake my head and smile in response. I went to see my mother on Sunday and worked the entire week, having odd hours which included early shifts staring at five in the morning or finishing some nights near midnight because of our extended holiday hours. Too-hot-to-handle, aka Zebb, and poinsettia potential (me) have been texting throughout the week, but his shifts are just as chaotic as mine with two days on and two days off.

Zaleya was stunned when I asked someone to switch a shift with me. Finding a replacement for a Saturday night during the holiday season was nearly impossible but finally a newer floor manager agreed to cover my last two hours so I could at least leave work early to shower and change.

Ducking into his truck without answering Zebb, he closes my door and rounds the front.

"So what should I expect tonight?" I ask, fluffing out the skirt of the costume and shrugging out of my wings for comfort. Plus, wings weren't conducive for putting on a seatbelt.

"Just a bunch of guys and their wives or girlfriends, talking shit and drinking too much. Only believe half of what you hear tonight."

"About you or just everyone in general?"

"Especially about me." He winks at me while driving to the end of my street. "We rented a pub. It's low key but it should be fun."

His radio is on and as if I don't hear enough Christmas music throughout the day, a song begins to play.

"This is one of the saddest Christmas songs," I say. "I'll Be Home for Christmas" streams through his truck.

"First you don't like Christmas. Now you're dissing the music. What is wrong with you?" He's teasing but he has no idea how often I ask myself the same thing.

"It's just that some people don't have homes to go to for Christmas."

Zebb is silent as he turns a corner. "I get that, but he does sing if only in his dreams."

If only . . .

"Yeah." I'm quiet after that, my lips sealing shut.

"What do you do for Christmas?" Curiosity fills Zebb's voice.

"Oh, I don't really celebrate." I smooth my hands down the skirt of my costume, not wanting to discuss the holiday.

"Come on. You must do something?"

I think back on the years where I've cooked myself a small chicken breast and fancied it up with boxed stuffing. Or the year I ordered Chinese to honor Ralphie and his family from *A Christmas Story*.

"My dad always took us on a vacation over Christmas. As I grew older and had to work, I stopped going with him. I'd just stay at home."

"Alone?" The censure in his voice says he can't believe such an idea.

"Some years I might have hung out with friends or a boyfriend." Although I didn't have many boyfriends over the years. I can only think of one or two times I'd gone with a man to his family's home. In both cases, I thought the invitation meant something more. From one, I later learned I'd been invited to get his family off his back about marriage. From the other, I'd been included to make a former girlfriend jealous.

As for friends, the collection has grown smaller and smaller as I aged. I didn't have a spouse, so it took me out of double dating. I didn't have children, so the circle contracted even more. I had nothing in common with newbie moms or their eventually-growing kids and the trials of adolescents.

"What did you do for Thanksgiving?" Zebb's voice is quiet, hesitant even.

My mouth falls open and then shuts. Internal conflict rages. Should I tell him what I did? "I usually go to a homeless shelter on Thanksgiving to serve meals to others."

Zebb slows at a stop light and glances at me from across the truck. "That's really . . . nice." But the tenderness in his voice is masked with pity.

"This year I visited my mother."

His brows pinch and the light turns to green. He accelerates but says, "I thought your mom wasn't in the picture."

"She returned. It's a new development."

He peers over at me again but doesn't ask more as I gaze out the side window. Thinking about my mother is such a downer. I went to see her this past Sunday. While there, I told her about my date with Zebb, leaving out what we'd done in his truck. She smiled at me as I spoke but didn't share any words of encouragement or advice. What did she know about second chances anyway?

"I'll probably visit my mother this Christmas." I try to sound cheery about the possibility but inside there is no joy in the probability.

Zebb doesn't respond and soon he is looking for street parking. Once we find a spot, he helps me out of his truck and then assists me placing my wings back on.

A large banner greets us as we enter the party.

"A Snowball's Chance? I don't get it." Zebb holds my hand again and I've wrapped my other hand around his bicep.

"We're firemen. A snowball doesn't have a chance in hell where fire reigns. Tonight is an innocent snowball's chance." He wiggles his brows as his gaze rakes over me.

"Ah. Is that a euphemism for getting lucky tonight?"

"Who knows?" He squeezes my hand.

The pub is loud and filled with sexy Santas and even sexier elves. I'm completely overdressed in my angel costume and opposite most other women here with their short skirts and buxom bosoms. Zebb stands out as well in his green velvet robe compared to all the open Santa jackets with a few bare chests exposed.

"What the fuck are you?" A deep male voice comes from behind us and Zebb turns as he's clapped on the back. *Another man dressed as Santa.*

It's starting to look a little like a Santa convention in here.

"I'm the Ghost of Christmas Present."

The man makes a horrified face and laughs. "Eek. You're scaring me alright." He lifts his glass and takes a quick drink. "Seriously, you look like Joseph who lost his Mary."

Zebb gives the man a scathing look, then introduces us. "Eva, this is Mick Schitt."

"No shit?" I mumble.

"Yes, shit," Zebb teases as the man looks at me as if he hadn't noticed I'm attached to Zebb's hand.

"It's pronounced shite," he corrects, rubbing his hand along a t-shirt that's exposed by his open Santa jacket.

"Where is the -e then?" Zebb scoffs.

"It's silent."

"Exactly, which is why it's shit."

"You're shit." Santa Mick mocks and glances at me. "How is an angel like you with a man like him?"

My face heats. Certain that he's referencing the costume, his question still feels like a compliment.

"Eva was the love of my life in high school."

I . . . *what?*

I tip my head to look at Zebb. When I see the expression on his face, I'm convinced he's joking around. Just like this exchange over the pronunciation of Mick's last name.

Right. Zebb is quite the Christmas cracker, full of glitter and air.

"Yeah, yeah. You and love. Get a drink. Fireball is the specialty tonight." Mick lifts his glass. "May we all have a snowball's chance." He eyes me over the glass. "Or an angel." He drinks and Zebb gently pushes at his friend's shoulder.

"Don't flirt with my date."

Mick dribbles beer down his t-shirt and roughly swipes at the spill before moving away.

"What a shit," Zebb mutters as Mick leaves us and we shift through more people calling out Zebb's name until we reach the bar.

"You made it." My head turns at the sound of Brock's voice.

"Your brother is a fireman, too?"

Brock reaches for his brother's shoulder and jostles him. "How he got the job? Little brother couldn't do anything without me." Brock's words are slurred and his eyes unfocused. He sways toward his younger sibling.

"Yeah, right." Sarcasm fills Zebb's muttered response.

"Think we're going to do good tonight, buddy boy. Probably bring in about fifteen thousand for you and—"

"Can I get you another drink?" Zebb interjects while Brock's glazed eyes turn to me. If you ask me, he's had enough of the spiked eggnog already, although I'm certain that's not what he's been drinking.

Brock lifts his beer like his arm weighs more than the glass and he salutes his brother. He then pushes off his brother and disappears into the crowd.

"Sorry about that," Zebb says, watching his brother sway away.

"Should you go after him?"

Zebb exhales. "Nah. He'll drink another or two and pass out in a corner."

"That doesn't sound good."

Zebb sighs. "It's a long story. He and his wife split about a year ago and he's not been handling it well, even though she was a bitch."

"I'm sorry to hear that." It's always difficult to hear of marriages failing. I'd definitely lost faith in the institution at a young age, but I did hope others might find a happily-ever-after even if it wasn't written in the stars for me.

When my mind comes back to the present, Zebb is ordering us two shots of Fireball.

"Oh gosh, I'm not much for shots." I still can't believe I downed one the night of our reunion.

Zebb looks over at me as we wait on the order. "You did one the other night? When we bumped into each other."

"I was nervous then."

Slowly, his mouth curls, one corner hitching up before the other. "Are you nervous tonight?"

"Should I be?" I match his smile. If he suggests we're having sex tonight, I'd give a resounding yes. But the truth is, it's been a while since I've had *relations* with someone. Other than Zebb touching me a week ago, it's been a freeze-out worthy of the North Pole since anyone has been near my personal Santa's workshop.

"You'll never have to be anxious around me." His eyes soften. His expression more somber. I don't know what he means but I nod as two shot glasses are set on the bar top. Zebb hands one to me and then takes the other.

"To a snowball's chance." He lifts his glass.

"To balls of fire." I lift my Fireball shot and toss it back. The burn waters my eyes. The cinnamon tingle reminds me of Zebb's kisses.

With his eyes on me, Zebb tosses back his shot. Then he slams the glass on the bar top and cups my jaw. The kiss is something I don't see coming. Fast and fierce, he's that snowball rushing through hell.

What chance does he want? Survival? A second shot at . . . us?

She was the love of my life in high school.

He didn't mean it.

But his kiss right now feels like I'm the air that feeds fire, and he's going to burn us both to the ground.

+ + +

The party plays out with loud laughter and rowdy renditions of Christmas carols. I can't remember the last time I had so much fun obnoxiously belting out *Jingle Bells*, which these firemen have changed to dirty lyrics, including a new title of *Jingle Balls*. Zebb and I drink and dance, although there isn't an official dance floor, and our movement is more like an embrace that sways out of beat with the music.

"Tell me again why we broke up?" His nose nuzzles the shell of my ear.

"Because you went off to live a dream."

Zebb pulls back and stares down at me. "No, you went off to another state for school."

I stare back at him, confused by the accusation. "We both went off to college. And summer ended."

"We could have stayed in touch, though." Zebb sighs, looking over my head.

Long distance wouldn't have ever worked. Besides, his plans were a little larger than mine. He didn't need a girlfriend in the way of reaching for the NFL. Maybe we could have at least remained friends, but I would have been jealous of every girl that came after me. She'd have what I didn't which was Zebb in the flesh.

"Why didn't we date before that summer?" I ask, curiosity getting the better of me. I'm not certain I want this answer.

Zebb scoops loose hair around my ear. "Because you were you. Quiet. Standoffish. Unobtainable." His eyes focus on where his fingers trace.

"You mean like a wallflower, standing on the edge of you being you."

Zebb's eyes meet mine. "What I meant is you didn't seem like the type to be interested in someone like me."

"Star quarterback. One of the most popular guys in school. Yeah, rough to keep my teenage libido in check." I scoff.

"You left off not good enough to attend IA and fighting every day to prove I deserved to be there."

My mouth falls open. "I never saw you like that. You appeared *too* good to be true."

Suddenly, Zebb's phone rings. He has pockets in his robe, and we've marveled at the ingenuity of putting pockets in a dress.

"Hey . . . baby." He stammers over the word as he stops moving. His eyes lock on mine a second before he releases me. Holding up a finger, he gives me the recognizable symbol for *give me a minute*. Then, he steps away from me and not only does the loss of his body heat send a sudden shiver up my spine, but the tone of that single endearment hits my gut like a brick.

He told me he didn't have a girlfriend.

He assured me he didn't have a wife.

But the sound of his sweet yet choppy stammer has warning signs blinking like a late-night stop light.

Red. Red. Red.

When a minute feels more like ten, I excuse myself from no one in particular because Zebb literally left me standing alone in a crowd of people I've only just met. Weaving my way through the now drunken Santas and the little helpers who look ready to take their snowball chance, I exit the pub and find Zebb pacing on the sidewalk, speaking into his phone.

"She was fine when I left."

Silence follows his concern.

"I understand. They just happen." He exhales and his warm breath sends a stream of frustration into the cold night air.

More silence.

"Okay. I just . . . I'll come home. Give me twenty minutes."

After another beat, he hangs up and bows his head. With his back to me, the weight of the world seems to rest on his shoulders. The Ghost of Christmas Present has something scary in his closet.

"Is everything alright?" My voice trembles whether from the chilly night or the fear that he's hiding something big from me I can't be certain.

Zebb spins. "Yeah. I'm sorry about that. I hate to do this, but I need to cut our night short." He averts his gaze from me and peers out toward the street.

I risk stepping up to him although the vibe coming off him says not to touch him. He's already touched me rather intimately, but suddenly, intuition tells me it was all wrong to accept his fingers inside me or his kiss against my mouth.

"Whatever it is, maybe you should just tell me." My voice grows edgy as I steel myself for the truth. His rejection feels like an unexpected snowball aimed at the face.

"My daughter is sick."

"Excuse me?" I blink. I swallow. I stare at him. In the ten days since our reunion, he hasn't mentioned a daughter.

"I really need to go. I'll take you home first and then—"

"If she's so sick, you should get to her right away. I'll just call an Uber."

Zebb straightens. His eyes finally meet mine. "I'm not sending you home in an Uber."

"Then take me with you. Unless you can't." The accusation is there. He's married, isn't he? He doesn't wear a ring and I've been duped into thinking he's available. The thought seems ridiculous even to my own head which designed it but I'm suddenly unable to breathe believing this as truth.

"I told you I'm not married."

"Well, what do I really know about you now?" I wave out at him.

Zebb steps toward me. "I didn't feel like shoving two decades into ten days."

I nod. It makes sense. It's emotionally impossible to squeeze all those years into a matter of days, but a daughter seems like a pretty big thing to not mention on day one.

"Maybe you should just get to your daughter." My voice drops as I cross my arms. It's cold outside in my thin dress and nearly bare shoulders, but the frigid air is nothing compared to the polar vortex suddenly between Zebb and me.

"Tam. Her name is Tamarra and she's eight."

I swallow around a sudden lump in my throat. He has a child. He loved someone enough to have a baby with her.

"How many other kids do you have?"

"Tam is an only child."

This statement makes me feel worse. I'm frozen in place, thinking of a little girl, with a single father, who is home sick and wanting her dad.

I'm trembling when Zebb's hands come to my shoulders and stroke down my arms. He sighs heavily.

"You're right. I need to get home. Do you mind making the stop before I take you back to your place?"

Stunned by his invitation to go with him, I nod once again, hoping the boy I once loved grew into a good man who loves his daughter.

chapter 5

We rode in silence to a street in the Lakeview neighborhood where homes are tall, skinny, and close together, but expensive. I hadn't even bothered to remove my angel wings, but pulled the seat belt over them, leaning against the flimsy wiring. I'm ruining the distinguishing piece of my costume, but I'll never wear this outfit again without thinking of the contrast in this night.

Zebb pulls down an alley and parks inside a garage. He doesn't take my hand as he'd done when he picked me up. Instead, he walks ahead of me, and I follow like an errant child. Like I'm the one who's been kept a secret. Like I'm the one who doesn't matter because he hadn't told me about something so huge, and so wonderful in his life. He has a daughter.

My emotions ping all over the place and all the parts of me lit from the party are now a strand of holiday lights with that one bulb blowing out the rest of the string.

We enter his home by a side door and walk up a few steps to the kitchen. The space is large with opulent, top of the line, stainless-steel appliances and an abundance of cabinets in a dark blue color. The room is beautiful, as far as kitchens go.

"I'll be right back." He tosses his keys on the counter and disappears into a living room. Harried thumps tell me he's climbing the stairs.

A few minutes later, softer steps descend and enter the kitchen where I've been standing, stunned by Zebb's silence and feeling a bit dejected.

"Hi." A teenage girl who looks like Marnie greets me. "I'm Eleanor, Zebb's niece."

I introduce myself by simply stating my name. I don't know who I am to Zebb. Old acquaintance? Friend? One-time lover?

"I'm really sorry about interrupting your date. Uncle Zebb doesn't go out much, but with Tam's fever, I didn't know what to do."

"Of course, you should have called Zebb." I offer her a tight smile. He's a father. He should be informed when his daughter is sick. "Are you at Immaculate Academy?"

She nods.

"Is Nick your brother?"

"You mean Football Jesus?" Eleanor rolls her dark eyes. "Yes. He's my older brother."

When we hear heavy feet thundering down the steps again, we pause as if waiting on Santa himself to descend a chimney.

Zebb enters the kitchen. Discomforting frustration fills his voice when he says, "Tam would like to meet you."

"Oh." My brows lift and Eleanor turns to face me. She smiles, almost encouraging me.

"I'm sorry again, Uncle Zebb."

"No, you did the right thing." He rubs a hand down her arm. "You can head out. I'll be staying home."

Eleanor smiles as Zebb pulls a hundred-dollar bill from his pocket and hands it to her. After giving him a hug, she heads to what I assume is the front door.

Without a word, Zebb turns toward the living room, and I follow. Dread fills me. *She's only a child*, I tell myself as I hike up the skirt of my costume and climb the stairs behind him. Dressed like an angel isn't exactly how one should meet someone's kid.

Zebb pushes open the door to a room aglow in pink. Pink walls. Pink comforter. Pink lampshade.

And next to the white nightstand are two little prosthetic legs.

The knees look like cups and extend downward to two tiny feet.

I quickly look away from them and meet the most angelic face.

"Hi." My voice cracks with nerves. Zebb's daughter is sitting upright in a twin bed with the sheet pulled to her waist.

"You're an angel." Her small voice is full of breathless wonder. Strawberry blond curls cover her head. Her dark blue eyes are wide and curious as she looks at me.

"No. I'm only Eva."

"But you look like an angel." Still awe-filled, she stares at me.

"You look like an angel," I tell her.

"This is Tamarra. She's my little devil," Zebb teases, brushing a hand over her long hair. He's lowered to one knee beside her bed.

She giggles. "I'm not a devil, Daddy."

"But you're as hot as one." His hand flattens on her forehead, palm down before he flips it and presses the back of his hand to her head, checking for fever.

She giggles again. "I'm not sick."

Zebb harrumphs as I scan her room. A Doll and Me doll sits on the floor. One specially designed with prosthetic legs. An array of doll clothing is spread around a toy bed while a miniature table nearby holds a tea set.

"What's your Doll and Me's name?" I take the liberty to step around Tam's bed and point at the collection of doll things.

"I named her Zuzu."

I glance over at Tamarra. "Like the little girl in *It's A Wonderful Life?*"

"I didn't watch that movie. I thought it was boring."

I smile. The tale is really more for adults. "What is your favorite Christmas movie?"

"*Rudolph the Red-Nosed Reindeer.*"

"Good choice." I pause and turn back to the doll. "Have you ever been to a Doll and Me tea at Ashford's?"

Her little eyes widen. "No." She shakes her head to add emphasis.

"I don't know if your daddy told you, but I work at Ashford's. We have a special Christmas tea party every year."

Tam's mouth opens wide, and she glances at her father before looking back at me. From his perch beside his daughter's bed, Zebb looks over at me as well. "That event sold out last summer."

"I might have an in." I'd wink but the mood between us is not playful. Instead, I turn to Tam. "If you'd like to go, I could get you tickets. It's Tuesday the thirteenth at three."

"Daddy, can we go? Please." Tam's little hands press together as she bats her eyelids. How could he ever say no to that face?

"The thirteenth? I have to work, Tiny Tam."

Tam rolls her eyes. "I'm not tiny, Big Daddy. I'm growing."

"Yes, you are, and too fast." He leans forward and rumples her hair.

"You're growing," she teases him back. "You keep eating all Granma's Christmas cookies and you'll look like Santa."

"Ho-ho-ho," Zebb bellows, making a good imitation of the man himself. With the wreath still on his head, and the emerald-green robe, he looks like a youngish Saint Nick.

I clear my throat. "If you have to work, I could take her to tea." I have no idea where the invitation comes from or why I allow it to escape before thinking through the invite.

Zebb stares up at me while Tam's mouth falls open. Then she's cupping her dad's face with her delicate hands and forcing him to look at her. "Say yes, Daddy. Please, please, *please.*"

"I could try to find someone to cover my shift." He puzzles the thought more to himself than to me or his daughter, but I sense his hesitation. Maybe he doesn't trust me with his little girl whom I've just met.

"I could get your sister Marnie a ticket instead of me. So you don't have to change your shift."

Zebb turns back to me, his eyes narrowing.

"I don't want to overstep." I lower my gaze, once again feeling like I'm doing the wrong thing.

"Marnie would probably love it." Zebb faces his daughter again. "Let me check with her."

Tam squeals and wraps her arms around her father's neck. "Oh, thank you, Daddy!" My eyes prickle with emotion and I look away.

"But first, we need to get you better."

"It's only a fever, Daddy. I'll be better." Her nonchalance and positive attitude are a wonder.

Zebb presses a kiss to her forehead and forces her back to the pillow. "Now, time for bed, Tiny Tam."

"Okay, Big Daddy," she teases him while slipping under the covers and allowing her father to tuck her in. "When I grow up, I want to be an angel like Eva."

Her serious tone makes my eyes prickle even more. How innocent children are, to believe they can be anything, including angels one day.

"If you'd like to practice, I could leave you my wings."

Tam's mouth falls open. "Won't it hurt to pull them off?"

I slip my thumbs under the elastic straps and snap them. "Angel secret. Wings are removable when we need to walk around as humans."

Tam watches me as I remove the wings and wrap the straps around the knob of her closet door. When I look over at her, Zebb is the one staring back at me. His eyes soften from the unfocused daze they've contained since leaving the pub.

"No flying though," I warn Tam. "Not every angel uses her wings to fly."

Tam empathetically nods. "No flying."

"Good night, Tam," I rasp, emotion still clogging my throat.

"Good night, Angel Eva."

Zebb quickly turns his head back to his daughter, gazes at her for a long minute and then kisses her cheek. "Good night, baby."

"Night, Daddy."

Zebb and I leave the room and this time I lead the way down the stairs. I don't stop in his living room but return to the kitchen. As he's let his niece leave, I'm going to need an Uber to get home, and it's time for me to go. Using the location finder on my phone, I allow it to plug in Zebb's address and then pull up the app to find a car. There is one eleven minutes away.

"You were amazing with her." Zebb pauses just inside the room as I stand by the oversize kitchen island with four stools on one side and a sink on the other.

Once I'm done with my phone, I look up at him. "Why didn't you tell me you had a daughter?"

Zebb sighs and leans against the opening to the room. He crosses his arms and peers down at his feet. "I don't know."

The answer is a cop out. He had a reason not to tell me and the only thing I can think of is he didn't want me to know.

"You were married. It seems like that should have come up as well."

His head pops upward. "I wasn't married." Irritation fills his tone.

I arch my brows, waiting for more of an explanation for everything.

"Mary was a girl from the neighborhood, the one I grew up in. She was a good woman and a family friend. During one off season, I'd been home, and we hooked up." Zebb sighs and attempts to swipe at his head before remembering the wreath on it. He tugs at the thing and tosses it to the floor. "She got pregnant."

He slips his hands into his robe pockets. He's silent a second, staring down at the discarded holiday ornamentation. "I promised her we'd get married. After the season. After the baby was born. She deserved a wedding, not something rushed. But everything went wrong."

Zebb continues gazing at the floor. His thoughts obviously lost in memory. "The pregnancy was difficult. Mary developed pre-eclampsia and was on bed rest. I couldn't be here as often as she needed me. I'd put football before everything. And then . . ." His Adam's apple bobs. "She died in childbirth. Total fluke. How does something like that even happen in 2013? But it did."

He exhales and looks up at me. "Tamarra's condition is called congenital limb defect. Basically, her legs didn't fully develop in her mother's uterus."

I roll my lips inward, fighting off so many questions.

"I had a million questions when she was born. Was it something I did? Something in my sperm from drugs I'd taken. Was it genetic? Mary had been sick during her pregnancy. Was Tam's condition the result of a virus? Who knows? I didn't care. I had this beautiful baby girl hardly bigger than a football in my hands and she became my purpose in life. Not tossing a ball. Not the millions of dollars. Not endorsements."

His shoulders fall. "Suddenly, I was thirty-one years old with a newborn baby . . . Tam is my world." He points up at the ceiling, determination and dedication firmly in his tone. "I walked away from the NFL. It had already cost me too much."

My eyes burn with tears I fight. Everything in me wants to rush him, hold him, tell him how amazing he is. But I stand my ground as an invisible wall builds between us.

"That pity right there on your face is why I didn't share all this with you." His dark eyes turn to coal as his focus narrows in on me.

"I… I'm not pitying you," I stammer, swallowing back the lump in my throat while blinking at the unshed tears.

"Yes, you are." A heavy pause falls between us as I accept there isn't a way to defend myself. He has it all wrong. It's not pity; it's—

"I'll take you home." His voice is as hard as his eyes.

"You can't leave her, Zebb," I remind him. "And I already called an Uber."

Zebb hangs his head. For all his earlier condemnation that he wasn't sending me home in an Uber, I'm exactly where he said I won't be.

And I'm also out of place in Zebb's home.

"He's one minute out," I explain from the driver tracker.

"Fine." Zebb walks to his front door, and I follow. He holds it open for me and I step out thinking he's ready to slam the door in my face. Instead, he follows me down the steps to the sidewalk.

The hired sedan pulls up and I step toward it, hating the turn this once-magical night has taken. Zebb doesn't approach me for a good night kiss or even an awkward handshake. He doesn't say a word and he's already backing up to the steps of his place.

"Wait." I hold firm to my spot on the sidewalk. "Just wait."

He stops. His expression is one of disappointment and maybe fear. I know I'm afraid. This can't be the end when we're only beginning, and I accept I must share a piece of me to explain my reaction to everything.

"It's not pity for you or her. I'm . . . it's all on me. I never had what I witnessed in there." I point at his place. "How sweet you were with her. How it's evident you'd give her anything if she asked. I'm selfishly crying more for me than you or her." Angrily, I swipe at an escaped tear, ashamed of myself.

"You have all I'd ever wished for. To love someone enough to marry her." I choke, my heart breaking. "A beautiful child is testimony to that."

I hate that I'm admitting all my hopes and the failure of not obtaining either of them. Quickly, I brush at my face and dismiss any more confessions.

"I meant what I said. I'd love to take her to tea."

Then again, maybe tea is more about me as well. I want the excitement of her little face, the warmth of her spirit, near me. She's the angel, not me.

Zebb stares at me and everything inside me hopes he'll step toward me. He'll break this cold wall between us and pull me into his arms. He'll kiss me like he did in the pub before all his friends and co-workers.

Instead, the driver beeps his horn, startling me. Zebb nods without another word, and I turn for the car.

Once again, I hate this holiday, and myself.

chapter 6

On the second Wednesday of every month, I have drinks with a new friend of mine, Amelia McCaryn. Why second Wednesday is hard to remember but we make it a firm date in order to seek human contact outside work obligations.

Amelia and I met when Ashford's had a meeting with Impact, a marketing firm where she works as an account executive. The meeting was tense as Jude Ashford sat opposite his father, Tucker, who owns Impact and rejected every marketing proposal given by the team. I was so embarrassed by my boss's behavior I reached out to Amelia to apologize, recognizing in her a woman roughly my age and working hard to make a name for herself.

I've hardly let Amelia order her first peppermint martini before I'm spewing about Zebb and how it's been five days since I've heard from him.

"He ghosted you?" She stares at me over the table in a small bar roughly halfway between her downtown office and Ashford's. "A little ironic, right?"

I bitterly laugh at her joke. "I just don't understand. My walls can be cinder block solid, but he didn't seem defensive about anything before I learned about his daughter."

Amelia sips her holiday-special drink, taking a minute to collect her thoughts. She twists her long dark hair into a knot at the base of her neck. At forty, she's the kind of beauty you long for because she looks twenty-something.

"Do you think he was hoping to just hook up with you and move on? Maybe closure or something." Amelia leans on the table.

"Closure to what? A summer fling when we were eighteen?" I fall back into my seat, exhausted from verbally spewing the story.

"You said he told everyone you were the love of his life back then."

"He was drunk." I huff and turn my head. The bar is packed for midweek and damn Christmas carols are audible over the din of conversations. "Well, not drunk, but drinking. He had to be kidding."

"But did he have to be? Are you sure he was kidding? Maybe he did have feelings for you." Her brown eyes narrow.

"He couldn't have." The retort is quick and sharp.

"Why not?"

I don't have an answer. Why couldn't he have felt more for me? I felt strongly about him. He dared me to kiss him. He stole into my room. I gave him my trust and my virginity. But I'm almost forty and none of that should matter now.

"Maybe it's like that movie, *The Holiday*, where the guy who's a dad just wants to be a man for a little while. He doesn't mention his kids, wanting to be seen as a sexual being and not a spit-up cloth."

"His children were older than spitting up in that movie and so is Zebb's daughter. His girl is this beautiful cherub." My thoughts rush to the angel wings I left her. Has she used them? "And besides, this isn't a movie. This is real life."

"In real life I bet single dads want to be seen as more than a father just like single mothers want to be seen as more than a mom."

Neither of us would know. We're single, nearly forty, and living in a pulsating city that shouldn't be lacking in good men. And the one good man I've found in years, no longer seems interested in me.

"Isn't there some rule about five days later?" I ask, as if I don't know that I've been shoveled into the coals.

"I think the rule is three. He should have called by day three."

See, no longer interested. I'll add it to my list of shitty things about this holiday season.

The problem is I was starting to think Zebb was different. Still that boy I'd loved and held onto in my heart, but presently a man who was obviously open with his feelings and confident in who he is. He was like an evergreen. You can dress up the tree in shiny ornaments and pretty decorations, but underneath the décor is a faithful pine tree with forever green needles and strong boughs. Where you learn things have changed, but at the core of the letter, everything is the same about that person. He is still a great man.

"Speaking of ghosts, have you seen your mom?" Amelia hesitantly asks.

"Yeah, every Sunday we have a date." Sarcasm fills my voice and yet I'm the one who foolishly goes to see her each weekend. Isn't that how it should have been? If she'd only stuck around when I was a child. She could have divorced my father, and I would have seen her every other weekend. Or maybe during the week. She could have been active in my life, if she'd only made a different decision.

And now she's back.

"I'm sorry. I know it must be hard." Amelia is one of the few people who knows my story. It's a classic tale of woman leaves behind daughter and then returns when she's an adult. Insert more sarcasm. I didn't read much psychology about such a thing when I took Psych 101 as a pre-requisite in college, but I am definitely the poster child for the chapter about abandonment issues.

"And how's your dad with all this?"

I dismissively wave. "Passive as always. Upset but burying it with the new woman in his life."

Our conversation shifts to plans for Christmas. Amelia knows I don't celebrate the holiday. With it forced down my throat for a solid month, I'm happy to have a day off and not think about Christmas. She'll be going to her sister's house in Michigan because her wayward older brother has returned.

As we're ordering a second drink, my phone rings. I'm so startled by the buzzing vibration against the table I'm almost afraid to touch the device at first.

Flipping over the phone, the screen reads: Ghost of Christmas Present. I changed Zebb's contact name when he hadn't called after forty-eight hours, the standard amount of time for a missing person's report.

"Answer it," Amelia demands, eyes sparkling across the table from me.

"I should make him suffer and ignore it."

Amelia sighs. "Or you can pull *off* your Grinch panties and just hear what he has to say."

"He probably just wants to confirm he doesn't want to see me again."

Then again, when Zebb and I parted that glorious summer, we never said goodbye. There were no lingering kisses or hanging-on phone calls days after our final night. We each stepped into a new life. Summer had ended.

When I think about it, he also hasn't said goodbye after each meeting with him. Not the night of the reunion or the morning he brought me the poinsettia. Not the night of the football game or after the party.

He hasn't officially said goodbye ever and it seems par for the course of my life.

My mother never said goodbye either. She simply walked away.

When I don't pick up the phone on ring number eight, Amelia reaches for it. Thankfully, I'm faster and breathlessly answer with hello.

"Eva?"

Shouldn't he know it's me? He called me.

"Hey . . . Zebb." Any attempt to sound casual is wasted as my voice cracks.

"I'm sorry I haven't called."

Uh-huh. I roll my eyes knowing he can't see me. I've had some doozy brush offs over the years. If pickup lines are bad, empty apologies and the weak excuse I expect next are the worst.

"Tam's fever was a little more than a fever and she was in the hospital overnight."

Guilt slams into me like a reindeer, head lowered and horns down. "Oh my God, is she okay?"

Amelia's head pops up and I motion with my fingers that I'll step outside a minute to complete this call.

"Where are you? It sounds loud."

I've just passed under a speaker piping out Christmas music. "I'm out with a friend." I should share that it's a girl and not a date but I'm still a little salty. Even if Tam was sick, Zebb could have called me. "Tell me what's wrong with Tam."

"She gets these fevers every once in a while. Just out of the blue. Like an episode of sorts. Most of the time they just pass but this one wasn't gone in twenty-four hours, and I panicked. They ran tests and kept her overnight but nothing." He exhales. "Every time . . . it's just fucking scary."

When I consider that Zebb lost Tam's mother in childbirth, something practically unheard of in the modern age, and consider that Tam is alternately-abled, I can understand his fear. He doesn't want to lose his daughter.

"I'm so sorry that happened. But she's okay, now, right?"

"Feisty as ever. She's been running around practicing to be an angel and even wanted to wear the wings you left her to make a snow angel tonight."

Snow has been falling all day. It's piling up and adds to the holiday scenery. It's also wreaking havoc on traffic. As I stand outside, a taxi blares its horn at another car where the tires are spinning on the wet pavement.

"Are you outside now?" Zebb asks.

"Stepped out to take your call."

He's quiet for a second and I can't stand the tension.

"I'm glad you called. Thanks for telling me about Tam. I'm glad she's better."

"I should have called sooner."

Ya think? However, I bite my sarcastic tongue. I get it. He doesn't trust me. Just like he didn't want to tell me he has a daughter or had a woman he once loved.

"If the offer for the Doll and Me tea is still available, Tam would really like to attend with you."

"With me?" I choke. A good choke. Like I'm overwhelmed by the sudden possibility.

"Marnie can meet you at Ashford's, if that works. I couldn't get my shift traded, but I think my sister really wanted to attend anyway. She's a teacher where Tam goes to school and handles pick up or drop off for me when I can't do it. She and Tam are close. Tam is beyond excited to see you again."

"She is?" I sound like an *eejit*, repeating words or surprised by them.

"I'd like to see you again, too." His voice softens. "I'm on duty this weekend, though."

"I don't keep weekend hours. I have to work myself. Busy season and all." I brush off the disappointment of not seeing him. There are other days in a week besides Saturdays, but I don't mention what days I do have off.

"I'm really sorry I didn't call." His apology sounds sincere as well as regretful, as in, maybe he missed me. That first week after the football game he texted me every day and told me he missed me after one week. Did he miss me again? Why hadn't he even texted me then?

"Zebb, you can talk to me, you know? Call me when you're worried or scared about Tam. I'm a good listener."

We didn't talk much about deep stuff as teens. With hands roaming bodies and lips meeting often, our relationship was more sexual, playful, and fun. Not that we didn't have issues to discuss, but that wasn't our focus.

We're adults now. We can do better.

"I should have called. Just hearing your voice makes me feel better."

I smile but don't return the sentiment. I do feel better as well but I don't want to let on how much I missed him or how hurt I've been that he hadn't called. Even if I now know his excuse.

Relationships need to be about communication.

It's one reason I'm not connecting with my mother even though she's returned. Our communication feels all one sided, which reminds me Amelia is waiting.

"I hate to cut this short, but I need to get back inside." The snow might be pretty but it's also cold outside.

"Hot date?" He brushes off the question with a chuckle, but the sound is edgy and strained.

"Just a friend." Again, I don't know why I'm not explaining myself.

So much for communication on my end.

When I return to Amelia, I explain Zebb's excuse and how Tam and Marnie will meet me for tea.

"See. Christmas miracle happening here." She waves a finger toward my face like a magic wand. "You're going to get laid."

"Oh my God, how do you get that I'm getting laid out of tea with his daughter."

"Because even if he kept her a secret at first, he trusts you enough to let her attend this tea with you now. He's shown you sexy man. Now he's opening up to give you his daddy side. If you can accept both, I predict all your future holidays will be filled."

I laugh. "Now you're psychic?"

She winks as she lifts her second peppermint martini in toast to me. "Call me the Predictor of Christmas Future."

chapter 7

While Doll and Me has their own store down on Michigan Avenue, Ashford's has a specialty collection in our toy department. With that contract, comes a twice-a-year occasion tea in our main restaurant on the sixth floor. At Christmas, of course, the tea is holiday-themed.

I have to work on the thirteenth but put in that I'll be off for two hours for the tea and add those two hours to the end of my shift.

When Marnie arrives with Tam, I'm a nervous wreck. She's only a child, I tell myself, but she's an important one. She's Zebb's daughter.

"Hey. Sorry if we're late. Last period is my planning period and I left as soon as classes ended. Traffic is crazy, though." Marnie is breathless like they've been running but Tam is calm as can be and hugging her Zuzu.

"Not late at all. We have assigned seating and the doors just opened."

The Tea Room is a highlight of Ashford's. Great-Great-Grandma Ashford's pot roast is still served on the menu during our dinner hours. The center of the room hosts a two-story Christmas tree with an electric train running around a track. The tree is always decorated in conjunction with a theme. Sometimes fairy tales. Sometimes holiday stories. Sometimes just an object like a Christmas bear. The idea is to always offer something whimsical.

This year's theme is *A Christmas Carol* which seems kind of harsh for children.

However, during this tea, the focus is all on girls, or boys, who love Doll and Me. Each place setting offers a little Christmas gift for both girl and her doll, plus limitless lemonade, finger sandwiches, and holiday treats.

I guide Tam around the giant tree and point out various objects including what we call the hidden ornaments.

"It's like a game. We give kids a bingo card where they can cross off the ornaments they find. If they find them all, they get a prize. Some are hidden to make it tricky."

Tam smiles, a devious glint in her eye, and I see the little devil her father mentioned in her. To my surprise, she takes my hand as we round the tree. The symbol of Christmas has lost its luster over the years but standing here, pointing out the ornaments and explaining the history of the room, the magic of the season crackles around me a little bit.

My heart isn't growing three sizes, but a strange sensation warms my insides.

"Here's our seat." I pulled some strings and begged Marcus, who organizes the tea, to give me a table next to the tree.

"Wow," Tam whispers once we sit.

"This was so nice of you," Marnie adds.

"It was my pleasure." I smile at Tam as our drink order is taken. Just like at Doll and Me, conversation starters are in a box, prompting guests to discuss topics or share thoughts.

"Your best Christmas memory," I ask Tam, reading off a strip of paper.

"This right here. But don't tell Dad."

"Our secret." I wink.

"Yeah, I don't think your dad would be too happy to hear that one. Zebb works hard to make this time magical." Marnie isn't admonishing, just laying out the facts for me. Zebb likes Christmas and it's his right as a dad to honor this time.

"Will you be visiting Santa and telling him your wish list?" I ask.

"Those Santas aren't the real Santa."

"Oh." I glance up at Marnie for guidance. Is eight too old to believe in the man in red? Or too young to stop believing?

"Daddy explained that Santa can't be everywhere at once, so he has to have helpers. Like elves but these helpers are extra special, like my dad. He dresses up as Santa and goes to the Children's Hospital each year."

My breath catches and I lock eyes on Marnie.

"That's right, honey. Your daddy is one of Santa's special helpers." Marnie runs an affectionate hand down Tam's arm.

Deciding against further Santa conversation, especially because I'm torn between Zebb as a sexy Santa and a man with a huge heart, we move on.

Mini-sandwiches arrive along with our drinks.

"What was your best Christmas memory?" Tam asks me. From the jiggle in her body, I assume her legs are swinging under the table. A sign of her excitement or maybe her ease. However, this question is difficult for me. I never attended a tea or believed in Santa after that fateful Christmas. The entire season felt like a farce when I was young, and I was definitely that kid telling others Santa wasn't real.

What a terrible thing to do to other kids.

"This right here." I tell her, smiling at her once again while Marnie watches me. Her head tilts like she doesn't believe me. This might be one of the first decent Christmas memories I've had but I can tell she thinks I'm just laying it on thick for Tam.

I reach for my tea and take a sip, realizing I forgot to add two lumps of sugar. Swallowing around the bitter taste, I set the cup down.

"When I was a kid, my mother left on Christmas Eve. My father canceled Christmas that year. I was ten." I catch Marnie's gaze before weakly smiling back at Tam. "I went on vacation every year for Christmas to warm places where it didn't feel like Christmas. So this really is one of my best memories."

Tam stares at me, surprised by my admission. "No snow for Christmas wouldn't feel right."

"You're right. It didn't." Christmas never felt like it sounded in songs or was pictured in books. It wasn't white or dashing or any other thing.

"My mom died when I was little," Tam says as if it's nothing.

"Out of the mouths of babes," Marnie murmurs. "Okay, new topic." She reaches for a slip of paper.

Marnie reads. "What do you want to be when you grow up and why?"

"Easy. An Olympic swimmer." Tam starts to move her arms like she's doing the freestyle stroke.

"Ever since she watched the Paralympics and saw Jessica Long, she wants to be a competitive swimmer," Marnie explains.

"She's my hero."

I marvel even more at this girl. "Excellent hero."

"Of course, Daddy is really my hero because he fights fires and saves people."

"Even better hero," I agree.

"What did you want to be when you grew up? Did you always want to run a store?" Tam asks all innocent, like I'm not already a grown up.

"I did want to run a store. Only a store that I owned. A bookstore maybe. Or a store that sells lotions and bubble baths. Or a boutique."

"You could have a store that sells all those things," she encourages.

"I could. When I finally grow up."

Marnie laughs. "Aren't we all waiting on that to happen for us?"

"Did you want to be a mom when you grew up? Daddy says you don't have any kids. I want to be a mom one day."

"Well . . . I . . ."

"Tam, remember what we talked about. Some questions are rude." Marnie levels Tam with a gentle rebuff.

"It's okay. I did want to be a mom. I mean, I still do, maybe one day." I'm not about to explain that becoming a mom, involves having a man, which I haven't had in years.

We switch topics again and dig into mini-sandwiches and cut-up veggies with a variety of dips.

Dessert is served.

"My favorite is the chocolate mousse with the Christmas tree cookie on top," I explain. The tree looks like it's potted in the mousse and the mousse has cookie crumbs on top to give the effect of dirt.

As dessert winds down, there's a call for everyone's attention to one corner of the dining room where a variety of young actors, who look like Doll and Me girls, gather to perform holiday songs from various cultures.

Tam asks if she can go closer to the corner and Marnie gives her permission. We can see Tam where she decides to sit on the floor with the other kids.

"I messed up telling her about my mom, didn't I?"

Marnie places her arm on the table and leans forward. "The truth doesn't hurt her. She might not need to know all the details but it's good for her to know that others have misfortunes and life goes on."

"Christmas is just difficult."

Marnie nods. Then chews her lips. "Look, I don't want to feel like I'm tooting my brother's horn. God knows, both of them have heads bigger than that tree." She hitches her thumb at the Christmas tree. "But Zebb really is a good guy. He hasn't been with a woman in a long time. He messed up by not calling you when Tam was sick." Marnie softens her voice. "He's never brought someone to the house to meet Tam before. I should know, I lived there her first three years. He wasn't keeping her a secret. He's just protective. He wants her to have the best life, everything as normal as can be, whatever normal might mean anymore. He doesn't want women coming and going from her life."

"I get that." I swipe my hair behind one ear. I hear what she's saying, and I understand.

"But what you might be missing is, he brought you to his house. He introduced you to Tam. He let her come here, although he might not have been able to stop her." Marnie laughs as she checks on Tam across the room. "I'm just saying you must be special to him."

I tilt my head, stupid tears blurring my eyes. "He's special to me."

Marnie smiles, giving me a reassuring nod. Then, we both turn our attention to the performance.

My mind races with all she's said but I can't decipher what any of it means. If I'm special, I still don't understand why he didn't call. But then again, I didn't explain to him I wasn't actually on a date.

Perhaps we need to give each other a pass on this bump in the road.

When Tam returns to the table, I sense a presence beside me and glance right to find Zaleya with a mini-cake on a plate in her hands.

Oh no.

"I heard y'all were having a party and I wanted to join your celebration," Zaleya's voice bellows loud, drawing attention to our table.

"Oh God, please, don't do this," I mutter under my breath.

"Did you know today is Eva's birthday?" Zaleya says, leaning toward Tam.

"Today is your birthday?" Tam's eyes are alight with enthusiasm and surprise. "How old are you?"

"Tam," Marnie warns as she did earlier about inappropriate questions.

"She's forty," Zaleya announces to our table.

I place my elbow on the table and perch my forehead in my palm. My face heats a thousand flames of embarrassment as Zaleya encourages everyone to start singing "Happy Birthday."

Tam seems to be singing the loudest, or maybe it's just that she's the closest to me. When the song is done, Tam encourages me to blow out the four candles on the cake, one for each decade, I assume.

I huff and puff, and the four flames flicker out.

And as sad as I thought the moment might feel, I actually don't feel too bad turning forty.

Not when there's cake and an angel singing in my ear.

Well, screeching a bit, but the moment is still rather . . . magical.

chapter 8

"Hel-*lo* Daddy." The salesclerk beside me mumbles as I'm helping her close out registers. We have a half hour before closing time and the two hours I intended to make up from teatime turned into four. "I want a lick of that peppermint stick."

My head pops up to who she's objectifying in the toy department when I see Zebb looking at something on a shelf.

The clerk is quick to circle the register station and head to Zebb. "May I help you with something?" With the twirl of her hair around a finger, she's offering him more than shopping advice.

Zebb gazes over her head and nods at me. "I'm here for her."

The clerk partially spins, pouts, and turns back to him. "Sure."

Was that word a statement or a question? Either way, Zebb's eyes are on me. It's been ten days since I've seen him and he looks amazing in an oil-skin jacket over another flannel shirt and dark jeans.

I finish what I'm doing with the computer and trade places with the clerk, addressing Zebb. "How may I help you, sir?" I bite the corner of my lip and Zebb slowly smiles.

"I'm here to buy a birthday present for a lady friend."

"A lady friend?" I arch a brow.

"Feels a little strange to call her a girlfriend at our age."

"Girlfriend? How long have you been dating?" I play along.

"We've been out three times but then there was this one summer when we were young…" He chews his lip while his eyes appraise my outfit. I'm wearing the red pencil skirt again and a thin-weight black sweater.

"She must be special," I tease, fingering one of the stuffed animals on the shelf beside us.

"She is, and I messed up. I didn't know it was her birthday."

I turn back to him. "It doesn't matter."

"Turning forty is a very big deal." He winks at me. "Tam had *so much fun*, her words for today."

My smile isn't huge but genuine when I say, "I had fun too. She's really sweet . . . and very eight."

He laughs with understanding.

"May I ask you something?" While I'm enjoying our little customer and clerk role play, I need answers. He nods and I continue. "Why *did* you let me meet Tam?"

Zebb tilts his head questioning my question.

"Marnie might have mentioned how you're rather protective of Tam and who she meets."

"Ah, but Marnie doesn't have a problem sharing my personal life." His laugh is bitter but not upset. "When you mentioned how you gave up your holiday for a soup kitchen, I knew you wouldn't judge."

I'm stunned. "Wouldn't judge? What's to judge Zebb? She's beautiful."

"I think so too, but people can be cruel."

"People, in general, are assholes. Case in point, this holiday." I wave around at the excess of toys we stock for this time of year.

"So I'm thinking this lady friend, who I owe a birthday present to, might appreciate something more adult. Where is the sex toy section?" He glances around before looking back at me.

"Ashford's is a respectable family store, sir. We don't carry those types of products here. And I'm certain your lady friend doesn't want to feel like gift-giving is an obligation." After all, that's how many people view the holidays. They must give a physical gift instead of something more important, like time.

"I don't feel obligated. I want to give her things." Zebb reaches out and swipes his thumb along my cheek.

"What did you have in mind?"

"Something that shows I'm groveling after ten days of not seeing her."

I roll my lips inward, fighting a grin. "I could suggest the women's department on level two. Or we have makeup on the first floor. Maybe an accessory, like a handbag. Although I've been told jewelry is good for groveling. Personally, I might prefer shoes."

"Shoes?'

"Who doesn't like a good pair of high heels?"

Zebb's gaze falls to my feet, taking in the shoes I've been wearing all day that are more for fashion than comfort and currently sending shards of agony through my feet and legs.

"Who indeed?" he appraises again, scanning up my legs, and climbing my body. Then he suggests, "Let's try the women's department."

I tip my head, implying he should follow me, and lead him out of the toy section. While we have an elevator that zips up and down our seven shopping floors all day and night, Zebb leads me to an escalator. As I step on, he steps onto the same moving stair and catches me around the waist, so I don't fall. Pressed into his body, he whispers at my ear. "By women's department, I meant lingerie."

My eyes close for a second, but quickly open again on the moving staircase. When we reach the women's floor, I'm leading him to the intimate apparel department before I consider what I'm doing.

As we near the section, the first outfit Zebb sees he pulls from the rack. "Respectable family store, huh?" He eyes the peek-a-boo red material with only a slip of black ribbon to be tied at the chest. A strip of white fur lines the two panels of flimsy fabric and wraps around the collar.

"Santa's naughty helper is more like it," I joke.

"Put it on." He holds out the hanger to me.

"What? Here?" I glance around us, but the department is empty of customers.

"You have fitting rooms."

"I thought you said you wanted to grovel." I hitch my hips, cross my arms, and stare back at him as he holds the outfit out to me.

"I intend to grovel. On my knees." His dark eyes sparkle. "Or if you want, I can put it on, and you can get down on yours."

As he holds the outfit against his body, I anxiously laugh, stirring up the sexual vibration between us.

This is one thousand percent against company policy. A worker trying on anything before her shift is completed could be grounds for dismissal, or at the very least, a mark on her performance file.

However, even though I was the consummate rule follower, for once I didn't want to follow every section of the employee handbook down to the subset of stipulations. Zebb was bringing out a side of me I hadn't seen in a long time. A side that quite possibly has been dormant for . . . twenty years ago.

"Fine." I tug the hanger from his hand and head to the fitting room.

My hands shake as I remove my sweater and skirt. I keep my heels on and wrap the barely-there fabric around myself, keeping on my bra and underwear. Taking a second to look at myself in the three-way mirror, I slide my hands down the soft material and then stroke my fingers along the line of fur. I adjust the ribbon which ties just below my breasts, accentuating them.

A soft rap comes on the fitting room door, and I jump, then giggle.

"Wanted to check on the fit, ma'am? How does it feel?"

"Zebb." I giggle again. He shouldn't be in here. There are cameras although they aren't technically allowed inside the individual fitting rooms despite the notice of surveillance.

The latch clicks open and Zebb slips inside without opening the door very wide. He stands against it once closed and stares at me.

"Fuck, you're a vision." His chest rises and falls as he stares at me in my red bra and matching panties exposed through the naughty Santa outfit. He's removed his jacket and tosses it on a chair inside the tight room. Then, he takes one step toward me, invading my space. With his hand on my belly, he moves me backward until I hit the cool mirror behind me. "I want to respect the shit out of you."

Zebb drops to one knee and presses a kiss to my stomach exposed through the opening between the two sides of the outfit.

"How do I get back on your nice list?" he mutters between kisses along my waistline. My abdomen flinches at the tenderness and I drag my fingers through his hair.

"Or would you prefer me on the naughty one?"

I softly snort, unable to think with him running his hands up my legs and his mouth sucking on my skin just above the waistband of my underwear. Zebb runs his nose along the silky material and lowers until his head forces my legs to spread. He inhales.

"Christmas candy."

I laugh. There's no way I'm— He licks me right over the damp material and my thoughts scatter.

"Zebb," I whimper, dipping both hands into his hair, massaging his scalp as my body quivers with desire.

"These past ten days have been an eternity, Eva." He swipes at the dampness once again. "How did I last two decades without you?"

I don't have an answer and thankfully I don't need to speak as he's dragging my underwear down my thighs while sucking at my hip. My panties are lowered, and his mouth moves to my center. Soft kisses. Sharp inhales. When he reaches my ankles, he helps me remove only one leg before he's kissing the inside of my knee and along my upper thigh until he has me spread wider. He blows a warm puff of air at my sensitive core and then laps. One wide swipe of his tongue and my head falls back against the mirror behind me.

My eyes close as Zebb licks and sucks, focusing on my clit. I rock against him, the rhythm a slow tap-tap-tap as he plays me like a drum. Rolling my head on the mirror, I catch a glimpse of us in the side panel. In excessive reflective panels, I see Zebb on his knees, his head slightly moving between my legs. The subtle bop is him devouring me. I peer down at him. He's looking up at me, eyes wide and coal black, full of mischief. He grins against me with his tongue stretched outward.

"Watching us?" He blows at the sensitive folds which are dripping with arousal.

I nod.

"Like what you see?"

My tongue is tied but a sheepish smile curls my lips.

"You're gonna be put on Santa's naughty list," he teases.

I reach for his face and skim my fingers along his jaw. "I only want to be on Zebb's list."

His expression immediately changes. Those dark eyes dance while softening. "You're at the top of the list." Then he returns to the business at hand. Two fingers enter me, and my hips buck forward. Zebb uses his other hand to pin me to the mirror. Held still, his fingers work in and out in delicious torture while his tongue circles round and round, and an orgasm hits me so fiercely my knees buckle.

Biting my lip, I'm afraid to cry out. We're inside a dressing room near closing time but all I care about is Zebb who quickly stands. Wet and musky, his mouth captures mine, kissing me like we have all the time in the world.

Pulling back, he whispers, "I've missed you."

"I've missed you, too."

A slow smile creeps along his face and then he spins me to face the mirror. "Look at us." His arm wraps over my waist and I lean into his chest. "Look at you."

My underwear is still draped around my ankle. With the naughty Santa outfit so revealing, there isn't much to imagine. Zebb slides one hand back down my middle while his other climbs to cup my breast.

"Red is a good color on you."

"I thought you liked the green dress." The one I'd worn the first day he came to see me at work.

He purrs into my ear as his fingers dip into my bra and his other hand returns between my legs. "Nude is my favorite color on you."

I laugh but I'm quickly silenced when two fingers enter me and the fingers on his other hand tweak my hard nipple with a sharp pluck.

"Zebb, I don't ever—"

"You will." His whisper is a promise. He's going to make me come again. With his fingers sliding in and out, making their own version of music, and his hand inside my bra, tugging and teasing my nipple, my body quickly reacts. I jolt back, rubbing my backside against his front, feeling the wedge within his jeans. My thoughts leap to the night in his truck and suddenly, I'm coming unraveled.

"That's it, angel. You're so pretty when you come."

I can't look at myself in the mirror. I can't concentrate on anything other than the miracle rippling through my body. I shiver. I quake. I feel so alive.

Zebb releases my nipple and reaches for my jaw, cupping it. "Look at yourself." He gently prods my face upward and I open my eyes. I don't recognize the woman staring back at me. With Zebb's hand between my legs and his mouth at my neck, I look thoroughly ravished. My lips are red from kisses. My eyes are wide and bright.

Zebb's eyes lock on mine in the reflection. "I've always thought you were the most beautiful woman I'd ever known."

Christmas crack, is he sweet.

And I want more of him.

Quickly, I spin, releasing his hand from between my legs. With a gentle push, I force him backward.

"What are you doing?"

"Tam told me you dress up as Santa and visit the Children's Hospital."

Zebb tilts his head as I press at his shoulders and force him down to the chair behind him.

"That's so sweet of you. And I want to tell Santa what's on my wish list." I lower to both knees and spread his legs.

"Eva," he growls as I reach for his belt, and roughly undo the buckle. Then I'm working his zipper. His hands come to his waistband and help me lower both his briefs and jeans to his thighs. His legs are trapped but he's exposed enough. I have what I want.

I wrap my hand around his thick shaft and stare at it as I stroke upward from base to tip. Moisture releases from the tip and I swipe my thumb over the slit. Spreading the substance around and around, I press a kiss at his hilt. He jolts in my hand.

"Fuck. What are you doing to me?"

"Gonna make you my personal peppermint stick." I laugh recalling the salesclerk's earlier comment.

This man is mine.

"Don't joke." He grunts as I lick up the length of him, squeezing the head before opening my mouth and taking him deep, straight to the back of my throat on the first swallow.

"Jesus, Eva." A tender hand comes to the side of my head, swiping back my hair. While he strokes through the length, I lift and lower, taking him in and out. I'm drooling and dripping all over him as his fingers tighten in my hair, fisting it at my nape. My pussy pulses again and I squirm.

"Touch yourself while you take me."

I shake my head with him inside my mouth. I can't. This is about him. And while I'm certain I could go off one more time, I want him to lose control. I want to make him feel good.

"Eva, you're gonna make me blow." His hips slowly rock and his hand in my hair tightens. I roll up on my knees, clenching my thighs together.

"Dammit. Touch yourself. You're right there and so am I. Let me watch."

I realize he can see me in the mirror. He's watching me take him and he'll be able to see me touch myself as I'm up on my knees. I spread and slip my fingers between my legs. I'm still soaked, and I circle my clit while my tongue circles his crown. Then I'm diving in. My fingers are frantic while my mouth sucks him hard.

Then Zebb is pulsing against my tongue and I'm unfurling like a ribbon pulled from a package. I swallow him down and ride out my own release.

When his hand loosens in my hair and my fingers slip down my thigh, I slide off his cock and rest my forehead on his knee. I just need a minute to regroup. To consider what we just did.

When I finally lift my head, Zebb cups my jaw and leans forward. "Happy Birthday, angel."

Whoever said your libido returns when you're forty, wasn't kidding, and this might have been my best birthday ever.

97

chapter 9

After our sex-a-thon in the dressing room, Zebb helps me redress as my hands still shake and my legs tremble. He takes his time to pull up my underwear and remove the Santa lingerie. He holds out my skirt and I step into it, placing my hands on his shoulders. Then he zips up the zipper. I reach for my sweater, but Zebb stands and slides it over my head, pulling my hair out of the collar. Redressing me might be more sensual than undressing.

Then he kisses me long and slow until the lights go off in the room.

"Oh my God, what time is it?" If the lights are dimming, the store is officially closed, and the night staff is here to clean.

"Time for ice cream. We just had cake." Zebb winks as he takes my hand and leads me out of the fitting area. "Thank you so much for your assistance. I think my girlfriend might like the gift."

"No more lady friend. Now she's just your girlfriend."

"Didn't put a label on her when we were younger when I should have. She's definitely my girlfriend."

My insides flutter like a snow globe turned upside down.

We take the elevator to my office where I gather my things. As we leave, I notice that Jude's office light is on. A pretty computer bag sits on his assistant's desk which I recognize as Bethany Cooper's, our Human Resources director. Like she was ready to leave when Jude called her into his office for one more thing.

"I didn't even ask you, where is Tam?"

"Eleanor came to babysit for me again. I promised her I'd be home by midnight as it's a school night, but I had to see my girl and wish her Happy Birthday. Why didn't you tell me it was your day?"

I shrug as we enter the elevator. "It's not a big deal."

"Turning forty is huge. You're entering a time of sexual rebirth."

"Assuming my sex life was dead in my thirties?"

Zebb chuckles. "I don't want to really think about you having sex in your thirties. With other men." He stares at me, those dark eyes returning to hot chocolate.

"Well, I didn't have much sex in my thirties, so there isn't much to consider." And funny he should mention a sexual rebirth because I certainly feel born again after *that* experience. My legs still tremble and I'm exhausted, but I also feel strangely invigorated.

"Be grateful you're forty, Eva. Some people don't make it that far." His words hit like a sledgehammer and are a strong reminder he lost someone he once loved.

I nod, preparing to ask him if he'd like to talk about Tam's mom. He could tell me who she was or what she meant to him, but then again, I'm also not ready. Not tonight.

With a hand on my lower back, Zebb leads me out a side door which employees use after hours.

"I could meet you somewhere for that ice cream, if you drove here."

"I don't own a car. I take the bus most days or walk if it's pleasant outside."

Zebb's eyes widen. "I don't like the sounds of that. You taking the bus this late. Walking home sounds worse."

I shrug. "I'm used to it. I don't live that far." Technically, it's only a mile or so.

"Tonight, I drive then." He leads me to where he parked on the street. When we can't find an ice cream parlor open this late, we settle on a drink in a bar a block from my place.

And I celebrate my birthday one more time with a shot of Fireball.

+ + +

Zebb asked me to dinner at his place. "I make a mean spaghetti from a jar."

On Thursday, I arrive at his house with a bottle of wine and peppermint and chocolate candy for Tam. She loves the Ashford's winter candy mix which includes chocolate squares with a crushed peppermint inside.

Zebb answers the door with Tam on his heels. To my surprise, he leans in for a quick kiss. Tam giggles and takes the candy to the kitchen.

"Wow. What a great tree." In the front corner of their living room is a Christmas tree that wasn't there before. "It smells amazing."

"Tam and I picked it out ourselves. One day I'd like to do the whole cut-down-a-tree ourselves thing."

"I never had a tree as a kid." It sounds pathetic but true. When you don't celebrate Christmas—for reasons—you don't have a tree.

When I glance over at Zebb, I smile weakly. "Don't give me that look." He's giving me the same pitying look he thought I'd given him about Tam. The difference is, he really is pitying me.

"I want to change your experience with Christmas."

I slowly nod, glancing back at the tree full of colorful mini-lights and glittering ornaments. "You are a little bit."

Turning back to him, he stands with his hands on his hips. He's wearing dark jeans again and a long sleeve thermal shirt. I'd like to tackle him under this tree, but I clutch my hands together instead.

"Just a little bit." He pinches his index finger and thumb together and tilts his head.

"Well, maybe a little more than a little bit." My face heats as I recall what's not so little on him.

"Wine?" he asks, seeing the embarrassment on my face. I nod and follow him to the kitchen but not before noticing two stockings hanging off his fireplace mantle. And just for a moment, I imagine one more hanging there. One for me.

Shaking away the thought, I enter the kitchen. "When did you get your tree?"

"On St. Nicholas day. We always get a tree on his feast day and then our elf comes." Tam squeezes her arms together. Her face full of glee.

"Your elf?"

"Elf on a shelf." Tam points to an elf sitting on top of their refrigerator. "He's watching to see if you've been bad or good. Have you been good this year?"

My gaze leaps to Zebb who is pouring me a glass of red wine. "I bet Eva has been very good this year." He winks at me.

"Daddy's going to make the naughty list again. He doesn't ever get presents from Santa. He swears too much." Tam smiles up at him from the stool she's climbed onto beside the kitchen island.

"Okay, Tiny Tam. No sharing all my secrets. Go wash your hands. Dinner is almost ready."

Tam scrambles back down from the stool. Her knee buckles, and for a second, she looks like she'll topple over. Then she rights herself and skips off to a powder room. I can't take my eyes off her prosthetic limbs. While I don't mean to stare, she's a marvel to watch.

"Her legs, as they are, is all she's known. She doesn't know anything different from how she is built and how her body works. The same as you or I can't imagine how it is to be in someone else's body."

"I get that. I'm sorry. I didn't mean to stare. It's just… She's so incredible."

"She is." His words are a touch of warning without a reprimand.

"You're really lucky."

Zebb tilts his head as if questioning my sincerity.

"I just mean, she's special. You're a good father."

Zebb presses his hands to the island. He stands opposite me. "Did you want kids?"

"I always hoped someday. Tam asked me the same question during tea. The issue hasn't been a desire for children. It's more a lack of the right man."

"And if the right man came along?" Zebb's hot chocolate eyes swirl.

"I'm forty. That ship might have sailed for me."

Zebb nods and we hear a door slam.

"Maybe I should have taken you out for a birthday dinner with a kid-free zone." He chuckles. "But I just didn't want to wait for another open night, and school nights are difficult to get a sitter."

I step closer to the island. "I'm honored to be here, Zebb. I don't need to go out to dinner. This might be the best birthday I've ever had."

He slowly smiles. "Well, there's more to come but first my famous from-a-jar spaghetti."

Dinner follows with a little chaos. Tam is talking, asking questions and giving answers. She didn't really need those question prompts at tea. She tells me about school and her Christmas concert coming up. She gets to play the recorder.

"Not the recorder." Excitement fills my voice as I touch my chest.

"Yes, the recorder." Zebb sticks a finger in his ear and shakes it while scrunching up his face.

"That good, huh?"

"I'm great at it," Tam tells me.

He shakes his head, mouthing *no*.

"Is it time for dessert yet, Dad?" Tam excitedly asks as we finish our not-so-homemade spaghetti. I'm on my second glass of wine and I can't remember the last time I felt so relaxed.

"I wanted to make you those mousse pots with Christmas tree cookies, but Dad said your birthday isn't part of the holiday. It's its own special day. Is it hard to have a birthday near Christmas?" Tam asks, all innocent.

"Yes," I admit. "While some kids get presents twice a year, like a birthday in July and then gifts at Christmas, I felt like everything happened at once." I leave off how I didn't really celebrate the holiday. I already messed up telling her about my mom which I mentioned to Zebb when we had my birthday drink the other night. Zebb said roughly the same thing as Marnie. It didn't hurt to tell the truth.

"The other reason we didn't make mousse pots is I don't know how," Zebb explains.

"I really wanted to give you snowman ice cream, but Dad said no to that too."

"What's snowman ice cream?"

Tam stares at me. Eyes wide. Brows almost to her hairline. "You don't know what snowman ice cream is?"

"No. I don't know what snowman ice cream is," I tease back.

"Dad, we have to have it."

"Tam, I bought a cake," Zebb says.

"But it's chocolate," Tam whines.

Zebb makes a horrified face. "Who doesn't like chocolate cake?"

"Me!" Tam raises her hand.

I reach for his arm. "I'm not a fan of it either." I feel terrible admitting such a thing, as he's gone through so much trouble, but I don't think I could force myself to eat a piece, especially after spaghetti.

"I'm a failure," Zebb mocks.

Stroking his arm, I turn to Tam. "But I am curious about snowman ice cream."

"Yes." She makes a fist and tugs her arm toward her body before climbing off her chair and heading for the kitchen.

"Note to self: Learn to make chocolate mousse. Second note: No to chocolate cake."

"I'm sorry. You're so sweet. It's the thought that counts, right?"

Zebb eyes me. "There's so much I don't know about you."

"We aren't those same teens anymore."

"No. But I want to learn. I want to know more about who you are now." His eyes scan my face.

"Same," I whisper. While I know the highlights of his story, who is he now, here?

"Snowman ice cream," Tam cries as she returns with three small packages in her hand.

"Bowls," Zebb says. Tam groans. "And spoons."

Tam returns to the kitchen but quickly comes back to the dining room. When I open the cold wrapping, inside is ice cream in the shape of a snowman. The frozen treat also once came in the form of a green tree or a pink and white Santa Claus. I haven't had these holiday specials since before my mom left. The memory hits me hard.

I slide the ice cream into my dish. Tam is watching me as I slip my spoon into the dessert and slice off a corner. The flavor is plain vanilla. Nothing fancy.

"Isn't snowman ice cream the best?" Tam holds her breath waiting for my answer.

I glance at Zebb before looking back at Tam. "Snowman ice cream is my new favorite flavor."

"Yes." Tam fist pumps again while Zebb gives my leg a squeeze under the table.

Tam devours her ice cream. "Present time."

"What?" I look up from my almost empty bowl.

"Dad said we have to wait until after dessert to give you a present."

"Zebb." Suddenly, I'm a little panicked. Dinner. Ice cream. It's already too much, but a present. I'm nervous I'm going to open a box with the Santa lingerie in it until I remember the item is still by my desk, waiting to be purchased. With the store closed, Zebb couldn't buy it for me. I told him I'd put it on hold for him, keeping it in my office for later. I'd planned on paying for it myself, keeping it as a reminder of what we'd done on my fortieth birthday.

"I hope you like it," Tam squeals from her seat as Zebb has disappeared to retrieve said gift.

When he returns, the box is huge. There is no small piece of jewelry in there or slinky negligee.

The package is wrapped in paper with pink balloons. Definitely kid paper but dragging out my birthday has been so sweet and too much.

A piece of paper with Happy Birthday written on it has been decorated by Tam and taped to the top of the package.

Cautiously, I tug at the wrapping paper.

"Just rip it already," Tam teases, elbows on the table as she leans toward me.

"Tam. Patience," Zebb warns.

With a sharp tug, I rip a large strip of paper to reveal the contents of the box.

No. It can't be.

Peeling back more and more wrapping, the image on the side of the box makes the contents clear.

"It's a Barbie Golden Dream Camper RV." My voice cracks as I read the label.

"Do you like it?" Tam's excitement floats over the table.

I brush my hand over the words, staring at the picture of the iconic doll camper pasted to the cardboard.

"It's perfect," I whisper as the box blurs. "Tam, do you have a Barbie? Maybe we can open this up and see how she looks in it."

"Yes." She nearly trips getting off her chair and then rushes from the dining room.

"What's wrong?"

"I just . . . . Where's the bathroom?" I ask although I don't need to use it. I need a minute and I step away from the table without waiting on Zebb's direction. I've hardly stepped into the hallway leading to where I hope is the powder room when Zebb catches my arm.

"Eva. Talk to me."

"Why would you do this?" My voice cracks again as a tear slips from my eyes.

"You said you wanted it for your tenth birthday but didn't get it. I figured your fortieth wouldn't be too late." He swipes at my cheek, brushing off the salty liquid. "I messed up again, didn't I? What did I do?"

I shake my head. "Why are you so perfect? Who *are* you?"

Zebb tugs me to him, holding me against his chest as my arms wrap around his waist.

"Why did you want that toy so much as a kid?"

I shrug against him, but Zebb doesn't accept the answer.

"Tell me."

I mutter into his chest which is warm and solid. "I just wanted to escape. My parents always fought, and I wanted to get away." I consider telling him about my mom and her return now, but the story is just so complicated. "When I was a kid, we took trips, but they weren't family vacations. Eventually, trips were getaways from the holiday. The camper felt intimate. Like something a family would do, where they'd spend time *together*."

My dad might have taken me away each holiday, but he'd tuck me in children's classes, or kid groups, and go off to do adult things. I was more alone on a vacation than I was at home.

"I didn't mean to upset you."

I pull back and look up at him. "I'm not upset. I'm overwhelmed. That gift . . . it was too much."

"Are you two done kissing yet?" Tam calls from the stairway.

"We aren't kissing," Zebb hollers back. Then he lowers his voice and directs it to me. "Not yet, at least. I really should have taken you out."

"Zebb." My throat clogs. "There isn't anywhere I'd rather be than here."

"Jesus," he mutters. "Now I really want to kiss you."

However, Tam is close, and she doesn't need to see us making out. "But not yet," I say.

Zebb gives me my minute in the bathroom to collect myself and then we spend the next hour putting together any parts that need assembly for my new toy camper. Tam drives it around the living room with her doll inside until Zebb tells her time for bed.

"Ah, not yet."

"Yes yet. School tomorrow."

Tam sighs but slowly stands.

"If it's okay with your dad, I could leave the camper here for you to play with."

Tam looks at Zebb, hope in her eyes, before turning back to me. "But it's your present."

"I'm happy to share." To my surprise, Tam rushes forward and hugs me where I sit on the couch.

"Happy birthday," she says with one more squeeze and the damn tears return to blur my eyes.

Zebb stands. "I'll be back in a few minutes." He takes Tam's hand and then swings her up into his arms. She's a little big to be carried but every little girl still wants her daddy to carry her sometimes.

I sit in the quiet of their living room and sip another glass of wine. Staring at their Christmas tree, my eyes lose focus. Tears blind me once again as I face what I've always wanted and never had.

I glance down at the toy camper. If ten years old couldn't be special, Zebb wanted to make forty memorable and he's done everything to perfection.

The dressing room sexcapades. Tonight's dinner at his home. His gift to me.

The universe seems to be teasing me and I'm waiting for reality to set in. For the moment where Zebb and I separate as we did when we were teens. Maybe he's just caught up in the holidays. I'm a project for him as he wants to change my mind about this season.

A knot forms in my stomach.

Zebb returns about fifteen minutes later and slumps onto the couch next to me.

"Does she go to bed that easily?"

Zebb sighs. "Yeah. She doesn't really need me to read to her. And although we have read some books together, she prefers to read on her own now." He scrubs his knuckles under his chin and his stubble makes a scratchy sound. "She's growing so fast."

I smile. I don't have much interaction with children other than the hordes that come through Ashford's.

"I don't know if you remember, but my dad died when I was young."

I nod as I do remember this about him.

"We didn't have much which is why I was on scholarship at Immaculate Academy." Zebb sinks a little lower into his couch. "But at some point, you have to let shit go. Like from that far back. Being a kid and losing my dad. Being a teen and being known as the scholarship kid. I get that it fucks with your head and hurts your heart, but at some point, you have to let it stop defining who you are."

I swallow uncomfortably and set my wineglass on the table before the couch. "I don't think we can ever erase what's happened before now."

Zebb's hand comes to my lower back. "Not erase it but accept it. It is what it is. Maybe it put us on a path. Maybe it felt like defining moments, but it didn't determine who you are. You determine who you are, Eva."

"Is this about the camper?" I narrow my eyes at him over my shoulder. His hand strokes up my spine and squeezes my nape.

"This is about your mom." He pauses, sympathy in his eyes. "In some ways, it makes sense why you hate the holiday. But don't let her do that to you. Don't let her steal this time of year from you. Don't give her that power."

I should tell him about my mom, but again, I don't want to talk about her now.

"It wasn't just my mom, though. My dad played into it as well with his bitterness and hurt. I don't know how to get around it. And where I work . . . Christmas is just so . . ." I hold up a hand and expand my fingers before my face. "So in your face."

"Have you ever considered another profession?"

"Retail is all I've known but maybe it is time to get out." I stare at my hands, clasped together near my knees.

Zebb tightens his fingers on my nape. "Whatever happened to you owning your own shop?"

I shrug, thinking of the business plan I'd once written up. The dream location. The perfect little store. I'd given up the idea when I came home at twenty-years old. I wouldn't be settling in some small town but remaining in Chicago. The plan still sits on a thumb drive somewhere.

"Some dreams change."

He should understand. He gave up the NFL to be a father.

"Or alter," Zebb says, leaning forward, pressing his shoulder to mine. The outside of his knee taps against the outside of mine. "I had football and I had Tam. They didn't happen at the same time, so I got to experience them both. Maybe it's time for a change for you as well."

I sigh, swiping a hand through my hair. This isn't a topic I want to talk about with him. He's already had it all. He doesn't know what he's saying.

His solid hand comes to my nape again and he jostles me. "Okay, no more serious talk during your birthday. Want to watch a movie? What's your favorite Christmas flick?"

I laugh. "Zebb, if you know how I feel about the holiday, you know I don't have a favorite movie."

Zebb eyes me before tipping my chin so I face him. "Pick one."

"*Serendipity*," I whisper. It's not really a holiday classic but takes place in the winter.

His brows pinch. "What's it about?"

"Fated lovers."

Slowly, Zebb smiles. "Then let's find it." He leans forward to kiss me, slow and sweet and too short. Then he's reaching for the remote, clicking on his television and tugging me back to his chest so we collapse into his couch and watch John Cusack search for a woman he lost but never forgot.

chapter 10

"Hey, angel." Zebb's voice is groggy as he gently jostles me against his chest.

"I fell asleep." I'm surprised as I slowly press upward.

With Zebb slumped into his couch, he'd tucked me into his side. Between the wine, good dinner, and the movie, I'd passed out. From his wrinkled expression, he did too.

"What time is it?" I ask.

He scrubs a hand over his face. "Three o'clock."

I twist to glance at the windows which have been dark since I arrived because . . . winter. But I still can't believe it's so late.

"Shit. I screwed up again."

"What do you mean?" I turn to him as he sits forward and braces his elbows on his thighs.

"I wanted to make out on my couch for a little bit." He sighs and turns his face to me. "I want nothing more than to take you upstairs and put you in my bed so I can hold you . . . but I can't. Tam isn't ready for that."

Or maybe he isn't?

"I get it." Staying the night is too soon with a little girl in the house.

"I can't even drive you home like a proper gentleman."

I chuckle at the reference. "Uber is my friend."

"But I hate sending you home in one."

I appreciate his guilt, but I understand his position. He can't leave Tam in the wee hours of the morning. "I'll schedule a car."

He wraps his arm around my shoulders and then I'm being jostled until Zebb is on his back and I'm lying on top of him.

"I don't think this is a good position for us," I tease as our bodies line up, chest to chest, legs along legs.

"I don't want you to go, though," he pouts.

"I really can't stay."

"Are we about to do this again?" His eyes dance despite the sleepiness in them. The Christmas lights on his tree are still on and the only illumination in the room as Zebb clicked off the television at some point.

"The song?" Again with "Baby, It's Cold Outside."

"We could mix it up," he suggests.

"I don't think I can be that creative at three a.m."

"Sure you can." Zebb pauses. "You really must go."

"I understand, though," I sing.

"But I want you to stay," Zebb croons and my panties melt at the roughness in his voice. If he can sing, I'm a melting snowman.

"Maybe another day."

"I had a good time." Zebb leans upward and presses a kiss to my nose.

"Why are you so fine?"

His brow hitches. "You're kind of a dream."

"I enjoyed snowman ice cream."

Zebb chuckles beneath me and not only do I feel that rumble physically, but the vibration resonates deep down in my soul.

"What about dinner?"

"It was a winner."

Zebb laughs again, jiggling me over him. He brushes back my hair and cups the back of my head. "You really should go."

"You said that before."

"But I can't reach the door."

"Then cut me loose."

"But I like your caboose." His hand slips down my spine and grabs my ass.

I laugh harder and struggle for a new line. "You aren't being fair."

"I don't want to care." He kisses my lips, soft and sweet, as his hand lingers on my ass.

"Zebb," I whisper in warning against his mouth as he continues to squeeze my backside.

"The only word I can think of that comes close to rhyming with Zebb is bed." His kisses turn more eager, and he slides his hand to my inner thigh, tugging my leg over his hip. I spread and straddle him, aligning parts that shouldn't be aligning if I'm leaving.

And I really should go.

"Bed and Zebb technically don't rhyme."

Zebb only hums against me as his kisses become more intense. I rock my hips, dragging my center against his hardness. His hand claps on the back of one thigh and he releases my lips.

"Okay. You're right. If I start this, I won't let you leave."

I rub my nose against his, loving that he's finding it as difficult to have me leave as I'm finding it to go.

"I had a good time tonight. Thank you for everything. The camper. Dinner. This." I lean down and kiss him once more and then I'm pressing at his chest, signaling he should let me up.

"Come to Tam's concert. I know it just will be a bunch of kids singing Christmas tunes, but she'd love to have you attend. I'd love for you to be there, too."

With my hands on his chest, his heart beats through his shirt. Sincerity flows out of him.

"Why now, Zebb?"

He tips his head and his brows pinch. "Why now what?"

"Why are you in my life again? How is it we're where we are? Me on top of you, on your couch, with your daughter upstairs."

"Maybe it's serendipity," he teases.

I roll my lips and slowly nod. My question was serious but maybe not a topic for three in the morning. "Maybe," I agree with him although I don't trust destiny.

She's been kind of a bitch to me.

And if I believed in fate, it means Zebb and I will soon part ways.

+ + +

I have to work the day of the concert, so I tell Zebb I'll meet him at Tam's school. Tam attends a Catholic school, and the campus takes up three of four corners on Addison Avenue. The concert will be held in the church across from the school building.

As it's the Monday before Christmas which falls on a weekend this year, my workday felt longer than normal. Getting to Tam's school, traffic is unbearable, and the church is a swarm of chaos as parents linger outside.

Zebb is waiting for me on the steps before the church entrance where he's talking to a woman who keeps touching his arm.

With his back to me as I approach, I hear their conversation.

"I was so sorry to miss you the other night. We really need to go out for a drink again." Her voice is full of seduction and innuendo. Whatever they've done in the past, she'd like a repeat.

What hurts is when Zebb replies. "Yeah, I'd like that." He scratches under his chin, like a nervous tick.

"I heard the Snowball fundraiser raised a ton of money for the organization. We need to celebrate your success." Her voice lifts, implication thick. She wants *sex*-cess. Excessive amounts of sex. With Zebb.

"Maybe before the holiday," Zebb suggests. "I'll call you."

I'm already in a crap mood but this is icing on a crumbling Christmas cookie. I've had a bad feeling since leaving Zebb's the other day at four in the morning. At first, I attributed the unease to a late night. I'm not too old at forty, but I'm old enough that an all-nighter before a workday doesn't work for me anymore.

Then, I saw my mother on Sunday.

In my excitement I told her all about Zebb and how happy I am that we've reconnected. I told her about my birthday dinner at his house and even the toy camper he gave me. Yet in all my enthusiasm, she only looked at me with pity. Like I could never have all the happiness I want.

Almost as if I didn't deserve to be happy because she'd never been. She'd been a bitter, selfish woman who left her child in favor of living her life. She didn't love me. She'd never loved me.

With this thought in mind, my feet are shifting. My brain is telling me to turn around and walk away until I hear my name.

"Eva" echoes over the chatter of people collected outside, soaking up the cold before entering an overstuffed church. Lisa is coming up the walk and before I can move, she's embracing me.

"I didn't know you would be here."

"Zebb invited me." I hardly recognize my voice. I'm numb because of the exchange I just heard between this woman and Zebb. I'm upset with the recollection of my mother. And I'm cold.

"Hey. I've been waiting on you." Zebb slips an arm around my shoulder and presses a kiss to my temple. I stiffen under his touch.

He just made a date with another woman while I'm here to attend his daughter's concert.

"Are you cold?" Zebb rubs his hand up and down my arm.

"Yeah." I'm fucking freezing inside and I'm so angry with myself for thinking Zebb and I were something special.

He leads me into the church, and we find seats which Marnie and Zebb's mom have saved for us. From our position, we have a clear view of Tam who is sitting with the other kids in her grade. She turns in her seat and frantically waves at us. I offer a little wave in return. Seeing her somehow adds to the growing hole in my heart.

What am I doing here?

"She was so excited you were coming," Zebb tells me.

"I'm sorry I was late." Or maybe I was right on time.

Maybe fate, as Zebb called it, had me arrive when I did to open my eyes and see Zebb isn't going to want to date only me. I look around the church, realizing most of the people are parents. They are couples and families. Zebb was teasing the other day in the store when he said he was shopping for his girlfriend. We weren't an exclusive duet. I wasn't part of a family. I was a party of one and I shouldn't be here.

Thankfully, the principal steps up to welcome the audience and with a fast introduction, the concert begins. From youngest grades to oldest, various classes perform. When it's Tam's grade, she turns as she stands to make sure her dad is watching her. With his phone held high, he's ready. Ready to document her life.

I don't think my father has a single photo of us together.

My mother certainly doesn't.

Melancholy washes over me like a heavy, wet blanket. I force a smile through Tam's performance as Lisa and Marnie comment about how good her class is with their recorders. Zebb chokes on a laugh, disagreeing with their assessments.

Zebb's mother leans over Lisa and Marnie to speak to Zebb. "There are many moments I've missed over the years, but the screechy recorder days are not one of them."

I offer her another forced smile. We've only exchanged a wave because of our separated seats.

Maybe the woman outside knows more about screechy recorder days. She's obviously someone's mother and sits a few rows in front of us. There isn't a man next to her but an elderly couple on one side and a teenage boy on the other.

With Tam's performance finished, she returns to her seat and mouths to her dad: *Did you see me?*

He chuckles as he gives her a thumbs up. They're so sweet together. He doesn't miss a moment.

She's the luckiest little girl.

When the concert ends, the sea of adults collect their children, and people make their way to the exit. Tam is holding her grandmother's hand while Lisa and Marnie walk ahead of us.

"Come over," Zebb invites. "We're having a little post-concert snowman ice cream. Plus, Tam has something for you."

"Zebb." I sigh. "I can't tonight."

"What's wrong? You've been quiet this whole night."

"I was listening to the concert." While some of the performances were amazing, my mind wandered until the older kids played a rendition of "Ring Christmas Bells." As the song rose in tempo, my heart raced, and my eyes fogged. I've heard this song a hundred times in a variety of versions and yet those eighth graders, clanging their bells in a church, were bringing me to tears.

"Come to the house. I can even drive you home tonight." He's teasing in tone but the reminder of going home in a paid car stings. It's a reminder of other nights with failed dates or faltering relationships.

"I can't."

We've stepped outside. Zebb's mother is leading Tam down the street. They must have walked here as the side streets are packed with cars and Zebb's home is only a few blocks away. I'm pulling my phone out of my pocket to order a car when Zebb tugs me down the alley at the side of the church. His big body presses me against the brick wall.

"What am I missing here?" Zebb asks. "You're different tonight. Talk to me."

I should mention the woman. I should tell him about my mother. I should say how I've had this nagging feeling about us since the other night, but I don't. He needs to get to his daughter. He needs to celebrate her concert. Make another memory with her. Relish the magic of this time of year.

"It's been a long day and tomorrow, I'll do it all again."

Rise. Work. Rinse. Repeat.

Zebb sighs, hands on my shoulders as he watches me. "Lisa and Marnie are going to tell my mom tonight that their adoption was approved. They're getting a baby. I should be there for their announcement."

Fuck. A baby? Adoption? I wish Lisa and Marnie every bit of happiness, but this is just one more reminder that I'm alone. I'm a forty-year-old, single woman without a family of my own.

Zebb's eyes search my face. "But something tells me I should take you to your place and we should talk."

"I don't want you to miss out on this important moment for your family, Zebb." I can't help but reach for him, running my hand down his dressy peacoat.

"Why aren't you ever wearing mittens?" He softly chuckles and cups my hand in his, lifting it to press a kiss to my knuckles.

"Go, Zebb," I whisper.

He looks up at me, eyes dark and uncertain. Then his mouth is crushing mine and he's kissing me hard and desperate beside the church. My fingers tug at his wool jacket and his hands are holding my jaw. His mouth is fire and brimstone and a statement of all the sins he'd like to perform with me.

And then he's pulling back.

"Goodbye, Zebb." I push his chest, and he steps back, but covers my hand with his, pinning me in place. His brow pinches.

"You mean, goodnight. Not goodbye."

"That's what I said," I softly respond.

"You didn't."

"I did."

We stare at one another when I don't correct myself.

Everything inside me insists this *should be* goodbye. I don't fit the picture of women who should be wives. A couple having a baby. A church full of families. It's all a statement to what Zebb deserves and what I don't have.

I weakly smile at him and slip my hand from beneath his, then walk to the curb and cross in the middle of the street, ignoring Zebb's call of my name.

+ + +

The night after Tam's Christmas concert, the doorman stops me upon entering my building. "You have a delivery."

I'm completely taken aback by such a thing. I haven't ordered any packages and I wasn't expecting anything.

Hosea points to a small Christmas tree, that looks like someone chopped the top off an evergreen and set it in a metal bucket. "That's for you." His voice softens, sweetened by the gesture.

A gift bag is also haphazardly tied to a notch where a handle would hook. Once I awkwardly carry the tree up to my apartment, I find a card inside the bag.

Angel,
Tam wanted to give this to you last night. She wanted to help you decorate it as well.
Hope it brightens your day. We missed you.
Love, Z.

Along with the note, is a collection of folded papers. Origami stars strung on a string and flat paper bulbs are decorated like ornaments. An angel has been made by curling paper into a cone and then wings and a face were glued onto it. The angel is bigger than the other items and intended for the top of the tree. A roll of fairy lights is in the package as well.

First Zebb sent me a poinsettia, then tulips and now a small Christmas tree with homemade ornaments.

I don't deserve him in my life.

Alone, I dress the tree topper, which smells amazing. Then I sit back and stare at the thing wishing my life had been different. Wishing I could find the holiday cheer others brag about and enjoy the seasonal festivities.

Wishing a black cloud didn't always overshadow this time of year.

the funeral

chapter 11

"Miss Nazar. This is Sarah at Benedict Care Facility. I regret to inform you, but your mother has passed on."

The unease I'd felt since leaving Zebb's place after my birthday dinner comes to a crescendo when I get this call on Christmas Eve morning.

Oh, the irony. My mother left me only days after my tenth birthday. And she left this earth days after my fortieth on the exact same day she first departed from my life.

I'd taken the call despite the chaos of Ashford's the day before Christmas. As usual, every man on the planet was *finally* doing his Christmas shopping and upset that the store no longer had in stock the *one thing* every man's wife really wanted.

When I saw the facility's name on my caller ID, I knew what the call would be.

"Eva. Are you alright?" Zaleya asks as I stare down at the device in my hand.

"My mother just died."

"Oh my God, baby girl. I'm so sorry."

I tuck my phone back into my pocket and reach for tissue to finish wrapping up a stack of clothing. I'm helping out again at the registers in the intimate's section as this is one of the busiest spots in our store next to jewelry and makeup.

My own personal lingerie is still at my desk in my office. There isn't going to be a need to play Santa's naughty helper.

"What are you doing?" Zaleya covers my hands, stopping me from finishing the standard wrap.

"I'm working." I state the obvious.

"Honey, take a break. Your mother just died," Zaleya whispers beside me, looking over my shoulder. "Why don't you leave for the rest of the day? I got you, boo."

"I need to work," I snap. My voice is loud and harsh. My hands tremble.

"Eva."

"Please, Zaleya." I turn to her, eyes dry. "I can't go home and listen to the "Loneliest Time of the Year" by Mabel or Tori Amos's "Winter" on repeat. I'll drive myself mad with my thoughts." I'd already done such a thing the night of Tam's concert. When I arrived home after leaving the church, I climbed into my empty tub and drank half a bottle of wine.

Would I be like my mother one day?

Sad. Drunk. Desperate.

"I get it. We all have our ways to cope but take a second for yourself," Zaleya softly encourages, removing my hands from the tissue paper and turning me to face her. "Allow yourself to cry. Or scream. Or something. Holding this all inside isn't going to help."

Her care and concern represents the love of a mother I never had.

I nod and excuse myself. Rushing for the bank of elevators, I enter my employee key for the upper floors, above the store are the management offices. Only, I press a button for the roof.

And high above State Street, I release a scream before bending at the waist and clutching my knees.

The cold doesn't even hit me. Neither do tears.

I'm all cried out for my mother.

+ + +

As the care facility is accustomed to patients passing on, they take over managing the particulars. My mother will be moved by a mortician. Thankfully, she already had a funeral plan. She wanted to be cremated. A memorial service will be held at a local funeral home. The sixty-minute visitation part of her plan is a surprise to me. Who would visit her? My mother had roughly three friends that I knew of and a handful

121

of nurses who looked after her. Then there was me. I had been listed as her only kin which is why I was contacted six weeks ago when she was placed in the facility.

On my abbreviated Christmas Eve lunch break, I scramble to make a few phone calls.

I call my father.

He expresses sympathy but not empathy. He'd long ago considered my mother dead to him. He won't be attending any memorial service for her.

"Why would I fly to Chicago during a holiday weekend for a one-hour visitation?"

To support me, I wanted to scream. But conversation about my mother was often a useless topic.

Then, I call Zebb.

Zebb and I hadn't spoken directly since the concert. He'd sent me the small tree and I'd texted him a thank you. He'd reached out, sending Christmas memes and encouragement to hang in there through this week of mayhem. He knew I was busy. He was busy as well.

He'd invited me to his mother's home for Christmas Day. Being asked to join his family during the holidays felt strange. Although I'd already met them all, it felt like a meet-the-family-as-the-new-girlfriend invitation. I didn't think I qualified for such a label. Zebb also invited me to dinner tonight, Christmas Eve.

To both invitations, I'd told him I'd have to get back to him.

For the twenty-fourth, I predicted work could run long and late.

As for the twenty-fifth, I wasn't certain I could face a family full of reasons to celebrate. This time of year has never been magical to me. I shouldn't have expected this year to be any different.

I had the perfect excuse to skip the holiday once more.

"I can't make it to dinner or Christmas tomorrow," I explain after greeting Zebb.

"Do not tell me you have to work." There's an edge to Zebb's tone. I've used the excuse often enough this week.

"My mother died."

Saying words to Zebb hurt more than I'd thought possible. Much more than when I'd told Dad. The silence following the rip of that particular bandage is almost deafening.

"Your mother? I thought she wasn't in your life."

I exhale, accepting that I never mentioned her return. "It's a complicated story."

"Tell me what happened?" The edge in his tone remains.

"Why do you sound mad at me?" My own tone is harsh.

"Because I care about you, and you've been blowing me off. Then you drop this bomb and I feel like you're keeping something from me. Something huge that might explain a lot."

"That sounds a little hypocritical," I mock, as old walls build like stacking blocks locking into place.

Zebb exhales. "I don't mean to sound that way. I just thought we'd already learned a lesson. We shouldn't keep things from one another. It messes us up."

"Because I'm so messed up?" I argue. The chunky barrier grows taller around me.

"I didn't say that."

"But I am," I admit as if punching at the thick wall closing me in. "I'm just fucked. And this time of year is the worst. And now, this." My mother's passing when I've been reunited with Zebb and had a glimmer of hope that things could be different. This holiday could be something other than it's always been for me.

Zebb exhales. "Why didn't you tell me about her?"

"Why didn't you tell me about the woman at the concert?"

"What woman?"

"The one flirting with you. She asked you to go out for drinks and you said yes. I heard you."

"What . . . Are you talking about Kaye?" Zebb gruffly chuckles and I fail to find humor in this revelation.

"I don't care who she is," I lie.

"She's Mary's sister."

Mary? Then I remember the mention of Tam's mother.

"The Snowball's Chance was a fireman's fundraiser. The guys decided to donate the proceeds to an organization Kaye runs to help underprivileged women receive assistance during pregnancy."

"She said the organization, like it's yours." I huff, still full of irritation but slowly settling to a simmer.

"I sit on the board of directors, but I'm not involved in regular activities."

We sit in silence a second before I exhale. "I understand. Mary was the love of your life."

"Whoever said that?" His voice cracks.

"She was the mother of your child." My own tone is reprimanding.

"Look, we obviously have a lot to discuss."

"I'm not coming to Christmas, Zebb," I counter.

"I think you should be here. You need to be around people."

"Don't tell me what I need." I have no idea why I'm arguing with him. He's trying to help. He's reaching out for me, but I don't need his pity.

"I don't want you to be alone tomorrow."

"No matter what day of the week, I always am." This is my lot in life. My voice is hardly more than a whisper as I stand inside my tight office. Taking a glance at my surroundings, I know what I need to do. "I need to work, Zebb."

"Don't do this, Eva." His voice lowers. His tone a plea.

"I've got to go."

"Eva—"

I hang up on him. Then I head to the closest bathroom and throw up.

chapter 12

Funerals during the biggest holiday of the year shouldn't be a thing. Even in all my dislike of Christmas, I don't wish this kind of sadness on anyone. Something so painful shouldn't happen during the happiest time of year.

And my boss is the ultimate asshole, lacking compassion.

The day after Christmas, which I spent with a *Harry Potter* movie-marathon and ignoring Zebb's calls, I approach Jude when I can't find Bethany, our HR person.

"My mother died. Her funeral is at eleven and I'll need to take an hour off. Two tops."

"Well, that's inconvenient," Jude states. He's such a cold bastard but I'd hoped he would spare me a shred of sympathy as he lost his own mother in a plane crash years ago.

"Don't be a dick, Mr. Ashford." I turn at the female voice behind me. Bethany enters Jude's office and I'm shocked by her abrupt entrance and her language towards him.

"Miss Cooper," he groans.

"Eva, you can take the entire day off."

I stare from Bethany to Jude and back. "No, that's okay. I just need a few hours."

Bethany approaches and reaches for my arm, rubbing up and down. "Hugger?"

Staring at her, I don't understand what she's asking. Then she answers for herself and pulls me into her arms, squeezing me. "I'm so sorry for your loss."

After a second, I shrug out of her hold, finding it weird that the Director of Human Resources is hugging me, but at the same time the gesture was welcomed comfort.

"If that is all, Miss Nazar," Jude addresses me. He's clenching his teeth and I bow like he's a king. Then I scramble for the door of his office. "Please shut the door on your way out. Miss Cooper, you may have a seat."

Yikes. I hope she doesn't lose her job, but something tells me Bethany knows how to handle Grinchy Ashford.

+ + +

I take an Uber to the funeral home where my mother's service will be held. I've already spoken to a social worker at the facility who will bring my mother's things to me at the service. She didn't have much. I went through her apartment six weeks ago, selling off her things after she was placed at the Benedict Home. The tedious process was like going through a stranger's belongings.

The process is also how I know she had photos or keepsakes to remind her of me.

As I enter the funeral home, I begin to shake. My mother isn't really here. There is no casket. A picture of her is set up on a stand. I have no idea where it was taken or who took it. She looks older than I remember her from childhood but younger than she was at sixty-five.

I stare at the image and take a seat. The room is too big to celebrate her life. I don't think more than ten people will show during this hour. The funeral home director already told me a minister would come in toward the end of the allotted time and offer a prayer. I had the option of a separate memorial once my mother is cremated but I opted out. I simply need to collect her urn in about a week. I have no idea what I'll do with her ashes.

As I focus on the image of my mother—a woman I didn't really know—I question myself.

Will I die alone?

What would an epitaph say about my life?
Did I enjoy myself enough?

I can answer question one and three easily. I need to do better. *For me.* Changes need to happen so that any epitaph about my life reads that I experienced joy and fulfillment. Had grace and forgiveness. How I loved and accepted love in return.

A single tear slides down my cheek and a finger swipes at it. I flinch at the touch from someone else's hand and twist to see Zebb in a dark suit sitting next to me.

"What are you doing here?" My voice cracks as I brush my other cheek.

"I'm here for you." Zebb's voice is quiet as he takes my hand and pulls it into his lap. He gazes over at the picture of my mother. "You don't look much like her."

"Most people would say I look like my dad."

She was pretty at one time. In my memories, from when I was young. But what she'd done to me changed my impression of her outer beauty.

"He isn't coming," I say as if Zebb asked. "I'm here alone."

"But you aren't alone, angel. I'm here." He squeezes my hand even tighter and lifts it to his lips.

"Don't pity me, Zebb."

He exhales, glances at my mother's picture, and then turns to me. "I don't. I feel sorry for myself. I knew this great girl once and I let her slip out of my life. Now she's back as a woman I want to know, but she won't let me close."

"I'm sorry, Zebb." More tears fall and they aren't for my mother. They're for me. This incredible man is sitting beside me, holding my hand, and I'm a hot mess.

"We can talk later." Zebb swipes at my cheeks again and tugs me against his side, keeping his arm around my shoulder as we sit and stare at my mother's picture.

"I don't know why she didn't love me. Why wasn't I ever good enough for her to stick around or make contact after she left? How does a mother walk away from a child?" I had so many questions I'll never have answered.

"I don't think it was about you but more about her. She's the one who had issues, Eva. Not you."

I know this in the back of my head and the bottom of my heart. I know what he says is true, but I'm still left to wonder, why wasn't I enough?

"I've been working so much, taking on extra time these last few weeks because I need the money. As next of kin, I'm responsible for all of this." I wave out a hand. "When she couldn't even be responsible for me."

"Eva," Zebb drones. "That's a thought for another day. We'll figure it out. Maybe she had insurance. Or benefits of some sort. But we don't need to think about this now."

"I'm so tired, Zebb."

"I know, angel. I know." He kisses my temple and tugs me tighter to him.

"I hate her," I whisper, waiting on thunderbolts to strike me down.

"No, you don't. You wouldn't be here if you didn't care."

"I wanted her to care about me. I wanted her to approve of me.

Zebb presses his lips to the side of my head. What could he possibly say to comfort me?

A few nurses visit. Two ladies I don't know pay me condolences as if I should know them. The minister finally speaks a few words about faith and forgiveness. His words blur together. When the service ends, I thank the funeral director who tells me they'll be in touch after the cremation. A box with my mother's final belongings is handed to me.

"What are you doing now?" Zebb asks as he stands beside me, arm around me in the lobby.

"I'm supposed to go back to work."

Zebb rolls his eyes and groans.

"But I think I'll call in sick for the rest of the day." I can't handle people rushing in to exchange items or searching for after-holiday sales. I can't handle people period today.

"Let me take you to lunch." Zebb squeezes me and I reach for my phone, calling Bethany to tell her I'll be taking the rest of the day off after all.

+ + +

Zebb drives us to a diner-like place. We order sandwiches and drinks at the counter, and then take a seat in a corner booth. The place is quiet. Then again, it is the day after a holiday and it's snowing outside. The dark clouds feel appropriate.

"Start at the beginning," Zebb gently demands.

"Six weeks ago, I got a call from a man. My mother's landlord. He'd found her in her apartment. She'd tried to kill herself."

Zebb lets out a slow hiss.

"There had been previous attempts." I let out a deep exhale. "She'd been at the Benedict Home before for mental health issues. I was listed as next of kin and contacted when they realized this time was dire. My mother wasn't going to recover or argue against informing me of her condition."

"So all this time, your mother was close?"

"I guess so. She just hadn't contacted me." All my life I'd struggled with why she hadn't reached out to me and all this time I hadn't known how much she was struggling. I wish I had answers for when her condition started. Was there a trigger or had she always suffered? As a child, I hadn't seen signs of mental concerns. I wouldn't have even known what to look for.

Had my father known? He'd never mentioned it, and for all his faults, the pain he felt after her leaving gives me reason to believe he'd never had any more hints than me.

Zebb reaches for my hands across the table. At first, I refuse his touch but he gently commands, "Give me your hands."

I stretch across the table. Although he held me to his side at the funeral home, I wasn't half as aware of his comfort as I am now.

Zebb squeezes my fingers. "So six weeks ago . . ."

"I'd go to see her every Sunday. She was in this catatonic state. Like she'd just stare at me. And I talked. I don't even know if she heard what I said." I sigh. "I'd tell her all kinds of random things. Like where I went to school and what I'd been doing. I told her how I hated Christmas and even that I blamed her. I shared stories from the store." I take a deep breath and exhale. "Then I started telling her about you."

"And what did you say?"

"How you'd sneak into my room. How I always felt connected to you, in tune with you somehow. How the instant I saw you again, that vibe returned. Or maybe it was just wishful thinking."

"Meaning?"

"We weren't those kids anymore. We didn't include feelings then and I shouldn't have them now."

"We might have never discussed our emotions, but it didn't mean we didn't have them." Zebb tugs my hands closer to him. "Being with you was the best part of high school even if it was after graduation."

"Why weren't we together sooner, again?" I joke without humor.

"I've already told you. You were you and I was me. And I was scared and stupid as a teen."

I stare at him over the table. "And now I'm stupid and scared."

"What are you so afraid of?" His eyes don't leave mine.

"What if I'm like her? What if one day I'm too sad to handle life? Or I end up alone which seems worse."

"Then you reach out for help." Zebb squeezes my fingers again. "I'm here."

I stare at him, wanting to ask where have you been all my life? But I have the answers. Living a life. Loving a woman. Having a child. Making a name for himself with his career.

"Why shouldn't you have feelings for me now?" Zebb's brows furrow as his voice lowers, and he stares at our hands.

I can't answer him. The truth is, what if he doesn't feel about me the same way I feel about him? I can't handle more rejection in my life. I don't want to be some project for him, like I was just a fling that summer.

Zebb focuses on me as if he can read my thoughts. "Mary was special. She was good and kind and everything someone should love. But I didn't love her like she deserved. For years, I wrestled with my own guilt that I hadn't loved her enough. I liked her a lot, but she wasn't the one. I knew that in here." Zebb pats his chest. "My heart was still holding on to someone else."

"Zebb," I whisper and glance down at our hands where he's linked his fingers through mine.

"Eva, call it young lust or first love but I hadn't ever let you go. And I'm fucking kicking myself that you've been in the city all along. I'd just assumed you were gone for good. I've probably been in Ashford's a handful of times over the years, and held fire and evacuation drills there, and missed you every damn time."

Our number is called for our order, cutting off our conversation. Zebb squeezes my hands once more before standing and retrieving the food.

I've hardly eaten the past few days, and when he returns, I stare at my sandwich, already forgetting what I ordered.

"I'm going to treat you like Tam. You need to eat four bites."

I softly laugh. "Why four?"

"One for each decade."

"Gosh, *Dad*. That's harsh." I scoff and pick up the sandwich. Taking a bite, the food melts in my mouth. I'd ordered roast beef with cheese on toasted rye. Something I didn't typically order but it tasted incredible. My mouth actually waters.

Or maybe it's just the man sitting across from me, offering a warm smile and steadfast comfort.

+++

After we eat, we drive back into the city. Zebb parks at my building but walks us to a bar a few blocks away. In the low light of a cloudy afternoon, we sit next to each other in a dark, wooden booth.

Zebb orders us each a shot of Fireball. "To the future." He raises the shot glass.

"The future," I repeat, feeling so uncertain about what lies ahead.

The cinnamon liquor coats my throat and burns my insides, but the after effect is a warm, sappy glow. A buzz happens quickly from a lack of food the past few days and the company of a too-sexy-for-his-own-good man, especially in a suit. He's removed his coat and rolled up his sleeves to his elbows. He still wears the tie and smooths his hand down the silky strip.

"Jesus that burns." Zebb laughs after he swallows.

"No snowball's chance," I tease.

Zebb nuzzles my neck and hums. "Speaking of chances, I didn't get mine that night."

"What about the fitting room?" Our eyes meet and his darken at the mention of that wild evening. His nose rubs against mine.

"I want a repeat." He kisses the corner of my mouth. "I want more than a repeat. I just want more."

The innuendo is clear, and I reciprocate his desire.

"Should we get out of here?" I ask.

"Only if you keep looking at me like that."

My gaze drops to his lips and then rise slowly to catch his eyes. "And how do I look at you?"

"Like I could be your world, if you let me."

He kisses me before I can comment. The kind of kiss that says snowy days, and lingering in bed, and snuggling under blankets.

Eventually, I pull back but cup his jaw, scratching my nails over his scruff. "What about Tam?"

"She's at my mother's for the night. Something about girls' night in, eating leftovers and watching princess movies."

"Sounds wonderful." I tug him back to me and kiss him quick.

"You'll get your chance but not tonight. Tonight's theme is this man in, as in, this man"—he points to himself—"inside you."

Holy snowballs.

chapter 13

When we enter my apartment, the moment is like I've seen in holiday movies, where kids rush downstairs to see what Santa brought. Zebb and I are on one another like each other is a gift and we can't unwrap ourselves fast enough. Coats are pushed off and tumble to the floor. I reach for Zebb's tie. He lifts my shift dress over my head. I undo the top buttons of his dress shirt. He reaches behind his head and tugs his shirt forward by the collar. Our bodies press together, mouths meeting as I'm sandwiched between his chest and my front door.

We kiss and we kiss until Zebb pulls back. He toes off his dress shoes and I work at his belt and unzip his pants. He lowers to his knees and removes my knee-high boots. He leans forward and inhales at the apex of my legs where thick tights cover me. I stand in my front hall in only a bra and the stockings.

Zebb slowly stands, shirtless and his unzipped pants hung up on his hips.

Santa Claus, is there anything sexier than a shirtless man with his pants unzipped and barely staying in place.

He grabs the back of my thighs and I squeak as he lifts me. My legs wrap around his hips, and he turns for my room which is visible from the front hall.

Our mouths reattach. My hands dig into his hair and his fingers clench at my backside as we stumble to my bedroom. When the back of his knees hit the bed, he lowers and presses me to stand before him. His hands stroke up the sides of my body before he rubs his nose between my breasts.

"You were a fantasy come true as a teen but you're a vision at forty." He sucks on my skin, and I reach for his hair, combing through the light brown strands. He's subtly going gray. He's going to be a striking older man. And I want to grow old with him.

Zebb pulls down one cup of my bra, the back of his fingers skimming my sensitive nipple. His mouth engulfs one achy breast then sucks to the tip, running his tongue around the taut peak. He blows on the wet nub, and I shiver. His hands skate up the backs of my legs and he pulls down my thick stockings. Once he reaches my ankles, I step out of the stockings and his hands reverse, skimming up the outside of my legs.

"I feel like a kid on Christmas morning. Excited and overwhelmed. Ready to unwrap everything at once. But also wanting to take my time. Peel back each layer of you and lay you bare to me." He doesn't mean just getting me naked. Zebb wants me, complex as I am.

"I'd say you've made a good dent in the layers."

Zebb reaches around my back, humming as he licks up my chest. "Time to remove more." He unclasps my bra, and Zebb pulls back to watch the material fall forward. He sucks at one breast while palming the other and then he shifts, flipping his attention to suck the right and palm the left.

Quickly he stands and pushes down his loosened pants. As they fall to the floor, he steps out of them, tugs off his socks and playfully pushes me to the bed. He follows me down, climbing over me until he blankets me with the warmth of his skin. His hand skims between my breasts, down, down, down, until he slips into my panties and right into my channel with two fingers.

"I'm going to make you mine."

"What if I want you to belong to me?" My eyes search his.

"I'm already yours." He removes my underwear and then shucks off his. We aren't using up time on foreplay. This is the reunion our bodies have been waiting for and we don't want to lose another minute.

"Condoms in the nightstand."

Zebb arches a brow but doesn't ask. He reaches into the drawer, pulls forth a foil packet and quickly covers himself.

Then he's at my entrance, staring down at where he holds his cock in his hand. He took my virginity when I was eighteen. Will he take something else from me at forty—my heart?

Or maybe I'm giving it to him.

This is my gift.

Slowly, Zebb slips inside me and looks at my face. Our eyes hold as he slides deeper, filling me. As he reaches the hilt, he pauses and brushes back my hair.

"Fuck. I feel like a teenager all over again. This is gonna be quick when I want it to last."

I nod as he holds still inside me. He kisses me, tender and sweet until I need him to move. I need him to finish me. Peel back the wrapping around me and expose the rest of me.

Sensing my need, Zebb releases my lips and unleashes himself. He pulls back from my entrance, teasing me with just the tip inside me before rushing forward again. Back and forth he works, building us both up. He skims a hand down between us, working his fingers around my clit as his movements increase in speed.

"Eva," he groans.

"I'm right there," I warn breathlessly.

He pulls back, teasing me once again with only the tip inside me. His fingers work more frantically at that sensitive nub. I whimper and whine, clutching at the firm globes of his ass, needing him deeper inside me.

"There you go, angel." He preens as if he recognizes the buildup. As if he remembers my body. "I want to feel you come around me."

His words tip me over and as the orgasm hits, he removes his fingers and rushes forward, filling me until his own body shudders and he's coming with me.

My eyes roll back as I praise all the heavenly beings and celestial powers above. My skin tingles, and my body feels indescribable.

More harking the heralds. And angels singing. And Zebb is a freaking king.

Then, he's kissing me again, slowly bringing us down from the high.

And then I'm falling asleep, naked and sated in my bed, with his arms holding me tight to his chest.

+ + +

I wake with a start.

My apartment is dark. My bed is snuggly warm, and two strong arms cage me in.

I shift and startle as if I'd forgotten that Zebb was in my bed.

"You stayed," I whispered, surprise in my voice.

"I didn't want you to be alone."

His comment sets me on edge when it shouldn't. I don't want him to feel sorry for me. "I'm going to get something to drink."

I wiggle out from under his touch and slip off one side of the bed. I walk the few steps to the front hall where our first scattering of clothing remains and I pick up his T-shirt, slipping it over my head. Lifting the collar to my nose, I inhale the scent of Zebb. Cinnamon and campfire.

And sudden sadness, something that has a distinct fragrance marked by uncertainty.

I pad out to my kitchen and fill a glass with water from the dispenser on the fridge. When I turn around, Zebb is on the other side of the island wearing only his boxer briefs.

"You're shutting me out again."

"I'm thirsty," I lie although the water does taste refreshing.

Zebb stares at me, reading me. "Earlier we didn't finish our discussion. The one about emotions. Not the ones from when we were kids. The ones we have now."

"*Do* we have feelings now?" I tip my glass in his direction before pulling it back to my lips, hating that I'm asking, hating the sarcasm that is a constant defense.

"You tell me." For the first time, Zebb sounds uncertain. Vulnerable even.

"Was this just a funeral fuck?" My voice is soft, cautious even.

"A what?" he chokes out.

"You know." I wave out at him. "You feel sorry for me, so we fuck. But eventually you'll go." I'll lose him. He'll walk away like my mom, and my dad, and even he once did.

"Eva, if you think this was a funeral fuck, then I definitely did something wrong." Zebb exhales and gazes down at his hands, braced on the kitchen island. Then his head pops up.

"You said yourself we had a connection, a vibe. We were in tune with one another. It's here." Zebb points between us. "Almost." He stares at me. "I want that girl again. She's inside you, waiting to come out again."

"I'm not that girl anymore."

"No, you're a fucking gorgeous woman." He huffs again. "A successful, determined, sarcastic, beautiful woman. Who works too hard and thinks she doesn't care when she does. I know you do."

We stare at one another across the island, and I set down my glass of water.

"You feed the homeless. You sat with an ailing mother. You're sweet with Tam. And you fucking fit me." He taps his fist over his heart. "And if you think we're just fucking, then let me make love to you."

"Who says 'making love'?" Tension slowly releases from my shoulders. He's standing in my apartment in boxer briefs. He's told me over and over he wants me.

I need to do something that doesn't come easily to me.

I need to trust him.

"Put me inside you again."

My body hums. I want him again. And he wants me.

But there's more in his request. He wants me to let him in—into my heart.

When I don't speak, Zebb shifts right but I break left. He rushes faster around my island, and I climb over the back of my couch which is only a foot from the stools on the backside of the counter. I've hardly gotten both feet on the cushions when Zebb leaps over the back of the furniture as well and captures me around the waist. My couch has an extended end and I squeal as he tackles me to it.

"There she is." He nips at my ear as he rolls me to my front. His chest covers my back. "My girl is still there."

Zebb shoves at the sides of his briefs until they slip down his hips. Then he's tugging me upward so I'm on my knees with my head down on the cushion. He's behind me. His thick tip at my entrance where I'm ready and willing to take him inside me again.

"You." He thrusts forward and we both groan as he fills me.

"Are not." He drags to the edge, hands clutching my hips. My fingers curl into the cushion and brace.

"A pity fuck." He slams into me and my body jolts forward with the motion.

I cry out but I love it.

"Touch yourself," he stammers through strained breaths. "Let me feel you again."

I reach for my clit, swollen and sensitive. Rubbing as he fills me over and over with his thickness, I burst around him. He stills, letting me ride out the orgasm on him. Then he's pulling free of me and flipping me to my back. He grips my ankles and brings my feet to his shoulder. Leaning forward, my knees bend and buckle. I'm open in a way I've never been. Exposed to him. All for him.

He surges into me again and I cry out once more at the fullness. Zebb stares at where he enters me, slipping in and out of me. The sound of friction and sex fills my small living area. Then Zebb stills and pulses inside me.

He leans back to loosen my shins which have been trapped under his arms. I wrap my legs around his hips, and he collapses over me. Then rolls to his side, keeping us attached.

"You weren't wearing a condom," I whisper.

"I don't ever want to let you go," he says, as if that explains everything. He pushes back some of my hair. "This is the best feeling in the world. This. Us."

He kisses me soft and short.

"I can be kind of a fruitcake."

"I like fruit and cake, so I'm not worried." His smile is soft, tender even as his watches his fingers trace back my hair.

"I'm scared," I admit.

His gaze drops to my eyes. "You think I'm not?"

"You could break me if you walk away," I confess, feeling more vulnerable than I've ever been.

"And the same would happen if you walked away from me." Zebb leans forward and kisses my nose. "I'm not going anywhere."

"You can't promise that."

Zebb stares at me long and hard and tightens his arms around me.

"It's called trust, Eva. You give it as a gift. And I take it with appreciation and honor."

I nod, glancing down at his chest, where my hand covers his heart which is still racing.

"Okay, Zebb." I'm still frightened but I'll work on my insecurities with him. It's my solemn promise to him and myself.

"Speaking of gifts. I have a Christmas present for you."

"What?" I blink as I look up at him.

"Tam loved the new doll and camping accessories, by the way."

I tuck my head. I'd brought over a Christmas present on Christmas day, but like a coward, never rang the bell, leaving it instead on their front stoop. The Adventure doll came with doll-size outdoor gear and outerwear for things like hikes, climbing rocks, and a swimsuit. The surprise was intended to go with the camper I'd left behind for her.

Zebb slowly pulls out of me and goes to my kitchen for a towel. He brings it to me, retrieves his boxer briefs and slips to my entryway. I tug a throw blanket on my couch around myself. Returning, he's wearing his briefs and holding a small rectangular box. We'd stopped at his truck before coming up to my place and his bag was another thing dropped in my entryway in our haste to undress.

"You didn't need to do this."

"Giving a present isn't about needing to." Zebb looks directly at me. "Or it shouldn't be. Gift giving should be a want. As in, I wanted to give you something." He knows my feelings about gift giving and the obligation of it during the holidays.

But I understand what he's saying and guilt washes over me. "I don't have anything for you." My brows pinch. "What kind of lady friend am I?"

I don't know what I'd give him of monetary value.

"You're my girlfriend, and I don't need things that come in a box from you." He sets the package in my lap, folds down to the cushion next to me and takes my hand, pressing kisses to my knuckles and then my palm.

I'm stunned by the 'you're my girlfriend' comment and stare at the brightly wrapped package is if it might bite me.

"I haven't received an actual present in a long time." The camper toy he gave me was the first present in wrapping paper I'd received in decades. My father used to send gift cards, which I didn't mind. Now he just sends money, which is still generous, but a statement to his feelings. He won't take the time to find something personal. He doesn't know me well enough to give me something meaningful.

"Open it," Zebb mutters against my wrist, which he tenderly kisses before releasing my arm.

Slowly, I unwrap the package, taking more care than when I ripped the paper off the birthday present he'd given me. I slide open the box and push aside the tissue paper.

A single mitten.

I glance up at him, confused.

"Serendipity. You like the movie because it's about lovers fated to meet again. This is a serendipity mitten."

I stare down at the fluffy hand warmer. "In the movie, it was a black glove." I'm not ungrateful just still processing what this means.

"This is our story, Eva. You never have mittens. But now you have me. We're a pair which means we talk to each other when things are tough. We count on one another for warmth, comfort, and holding hands." Zebb lifts the mitten and slips it onto my hand.

"I'm your serendipity and you're mine."

chapter 14

We make love, as Zebb calls it, one more time before morning with tongue and teeth and exploring fingers. The entire experience is sensual and maddening as I realize how much I've missed his body and him.

Then I tell myself, no more looking back. The future awaits us, and I have some changes to make.

We linger in my kitchen before Zebb will leave and I head to work. He picks up a packet of paper on my kitchen island.

"What's this?"

I take the thick stack from his hand. "It's an old business plan. I'd been reviewing it." I shrug. "I always wanted to be my own boss. I had a ten-year plan, but I might want to start that plan sooner rather than later."

"This is exciting." Zebb pulls the papers back from me and thumbs through the pages. "What do you hope to open?"

"While retail can be difficult, I still want a specialty shop. Something that has novelty books, homemade soaps and bath products. Maybe some housewares and boutique-like clothing. I was actually thinking of making it not-for-profit and donating the proceeds to a worthy organization."

Zebb's head pops up. "Eva, that's incredible. Do you know where you'd put it? What you'd call it? When would you open if you did it sooner?"

I laugh at his enthusiasm. "I don't know. That's one reason why I was reviewing the plan. Some of my initial ideas have changed after working at Ashford's for so long. I'd even change the business name. If I can work out a loan and find a location, I'd love to open by next

Christmas." Just admitting all that makes it feel equal parts impossible and exciting.

"I absolutely think you should do this." Zebb tosses the plan back to the island. "I'll help you in any way I can." He pulls me into his arms and kisses me. Just when I think I might get used to his kisses, he kisses me in a new way, and I fall for him all over again.

I'll never take kissing this man for granted.

+ + +

When I walk into Ashford's, I'm on a high from Zebb-sex and his enthusiasm for my business plan. Maybe being forty means it's time for a change. That's something Dr. Seuss should have written in a more adult book.

Maybe being forty, he thought, shouldn't make me feel blue.
Maybe mid-life was a turning point for something new.

Thinking these thoughts, I'm startled when Jude enters my office and asks me to meet him in his.

Stepping into his domain, Bethany is also seated before Jude's desk. He doesn't take a seat behind the imposing wood furniture rumored to have been his great-grandfather's desk but leans on the front of it and points at the chair next to Bethany.

"Miss Cooper has insisted on being present for this conversation."

Instantly, the baby hairs on the back of my neck rise. This cannot be good. While most businesses fire people before Christmas in order to skip out on giving bonuses, Ashford's lets employees go after the season. However, I've worked here for eight years as a full-time employee. I'm not seasonal help.

"We'd like to discuss with you something we saw on the surveillance cameras back on December thirteenth."

I wrack my brain but instantly land on my birthday and what might be on a security camera.

"You were seen with a non-employee after hours in the store," Jude says, lifting up a piece of paper.

"We didn't have sex in a fitting room," I blurt.

Jude's mouth falls open.

Bethany shifts in the chair beside me. Her hands clutch the arm. "Eva, I suggest you stop talking."

"You had sex in a fitting room?" Jude asks, his expression aghast.

I blink. "We didn't have sex. We just—"

"Stop." Bethany holds up a hand. "We are not hearing this."

"Oh no, I'd like to hear this. I'd very much like to hear this." Jude's lips slowly curl, but he doesn't look half as angry as curious. *Pervert.*

"Eva," Bethany begins. "You were called in here because there was a discrepancy in the toy department register on that night. You were the person logged in on the register when it happened. However, there have been two other nights of discrepancy in the same department, each with a different manager's login. We wanted to offer you the benefit of the doubt to explain yourself."

"The toy department?" I think back, and then I remember that I'd been closing out the register when Zebb entered the department. I'd been side-tracked by his presence, and we left the area. Had I gone back to log myself off the computer? I couldn't remember.

I didn't want to unfairly accuse a fellow worker, but the inconsistency of managers didn't add up. Jude needed to be looking at which salesclerk was working on those nights.

Then something occurs to me. "Are you suggesting I stole from Ashford's?" I glance from Bethany to Jude.

"Miss Cooper believes we should let you explain yourself, but I'd like more of an explanation for your fitting room shenanigans."

"Shenanigans?" Bethany laughs. "Are you eighty?"

I swear only she can talk to this man like that.

"Miss Cooper," Jude warns.

"We aren't suggesting you stole the money," Bethany says. "And certainly, being in a fitting room at the time of the theft gives you an alibi."

My brain runs rampant. "Did you think the person with me did the stealing?"

"We couldn't be certain. But if the man was in the fitting room with you, then it rules him out as well."

"He was with me," I admit as well, defending him. Zebb wouldn't steal any more than I would.

"And now, we have something new to investigate with you," Jude says.

I've worked long, tedious hours for this company. I've been a faithful employee for eight long years, and he wants to investigate me. First accusing me of theft and now this . . . this other thing . . .

"As you know, having relations in a fitting room is against—"

"I quit," I blurt.

"You weren't really going to go there, were you?" Bethany narrows her eyes at Jude. "You, of all people." There's suggestion in her tone and I glance from her to Jude and back.

"Miss Cooper, do I need to remind you I'm the owner of this company and your boss as well?"

"Nope. You do it all the time." Bethany stands. "As for Eva . . ." She turns to me. "Your record and devotion to Ashford's has been impeccable. We'd be fools to let you leave us."

"But you're firing me," I cut her off.

"Possibly," Jude says.

"No," Bethany interjects over him. "Your mother died, and you didn't take the bereavement leave we allow our employees. You're allotted five days. In addition, you've never taken a sick day or a vacation day this year. We owe you three weeks of time after eight years of service. I'd like to suggest you take a month off."

"So a leave of absence, disguising that I'm being fired?" My brows crease as I ask for clarification.

"We aren't firing you," Bethany corrects.

"We are," Jude states.

Bethany shakes her head and holds up a hand to Jude before looking back to me. "You deserve the time. You've worked hard. And if you did have sex in the fitting room, it isn't grounds for termination." Bethany narrows her eyes and glares at Jude, emphasizing her words. "But it would go down in your record for disorderly conduct. However, we didn't come in here knowing that happened and I didn't hear you mention sex. You specifically said you didn't have sex. I don't need to know what you did do. We wanted to discuss the cash drawer being short."

"But you're asking me about it two weeks after it happened." I look from Bethany to Jude, who hangs his head, and I realize something.

Jude needs me, not the other way around. I've been the top manager for three years under his shitty reign. He needs me to upkeep the reputation of Ashford's because he certainly isn't an asset. He might have inherited this company and been bitter about it but the people who work for him do it with pride because Ashford's is an icon in Chicago. He needs his employees more than we need him.

"I'm still quitting." I can't believe I'm doing this.

After eight years, and at forty years old, I'm walking away.

"Eva, I'd like you to reconsider. Take this month and think about it. We value you at Ashford's." Bethany keeps her gaze on me.

"Do you?" I direct my question to Jude. "Do you know the long hours I've put in? The things I've given up to work here? The life I haven't led because I'm always working."

Jude doesn't respond but Bethany's eyes soften.

She glances at Jude, pursing her lips before looking back at me. "I'm not accepting your resignation. Take your month."

"As a leave of absence? While you investigate me?" My voice rises with disbelief and anger.

Bethany shakes her head, but Jude doesn't look at me. This miser of a man who has a heart as small as the Grinch himself is a fucking coward.

"Good luck with your store, Mr. Ashford." With that, I turn away from both of them and walk to my desk. Staring down at it, I don't have any personal effects. No family photos. No cute pencil holder. Not even a plant. My office is plain just like my life has been.

I log myself out of my computer and exit Ashford's.

As I stand on State Street, wondering what I'll do with myself, I tuck my hands in my jacket and walk. Aimlessly, I wander through the theatre district and among stores. The street is slushy from yesterday's snow. The air is cold but my blood races within me. I start to sweat until I find myself standing before Old Saint Pat's, an iconic Catholic church.

I'm no longer a practicing Catholic and I debate entering the church. I stare at the heavy wooden doors and peer up at the steeple. During business hours, the church is open for people to wander in and offer a prayer. Maybe for good fortune. Maybe for business success. Maybe for something different.

I make my own silent statement standing on the street.

I will forgive the past, stop doubting the future, and love myself and others more in the present.

Taking in a large gulp of the wintery air, I smile to myself, resolute in my plan. Then I turn on my heels and walk in the direction of my apartment.

+ + +

"Hello?" I answer my phone when I see fox-of-a-fireman on my caller ID. I laugh as I hadn't changed Zebb's name so he must have done it.

"Hey. I didn't expect you to answer. I could have sent a text, but I like hearing your voice on the voice mail." *He's so cheesy.* "Anyway, I was going to leave a message. Dinner tomorrow at my place? I'm not taking work as an excuse."

"Actually, I just quit. Or maybe I was fired."

"What?"

"I was called into Jude's office. They thought I'd stolen money. Then they thought *you* stole money. Then I admitted we were in a dressing room, and I thought I was fired. So I quit. Then they gave me a month off." I squint up at my building as I near it.

"Whoa. Slow down." Zebb exhales. "Was this because of us in the fitting room?"

"Maybe." I'm not even certain what the accusation was.

"Shit. I'm so sorry. No more dressing rooms." Zebb weakly laughs. Silence fills the line as I enter my building. "I have furlough for the next two weeks. It's a mandatory time off. Let's do something during it."

"Like what?" I ask as I stand outside the elevator knowing I'll lose connection once I enter the box.

"I'll pick you up later today. Say five o'clock?"

"Okay." I don't know what he has in mind but I'm ready to follow him anywhere.

Once I enter my apartment, my gaze falls on the business plan Zebb tossed onto my kitchen island and the rest of my day has a new goal.

Today, I turn over a new leaf in my life.

chapter 15

Zebb texts me when he's downstairs. I exit my place, head to the lobby and step outside. Looking left and then right, I don't see his truck. A large RV bus is parked directly in front of my building.

Suddenly, the door opens.

"Hello, angel." Zebb sits in the driver seat and then he stands. As he walks down the steps to the street, Tam peeks around the edge of the door.

"What's this?" I chuckle as Zebb steps closer to me, and I tug at the edges of his open flannel shirt. He isn't wearing a jacket again.

"This is the plan for two weeks. A real Golden Camper RV. A real vacation." Zebb turns and waves at the large bus.

"With a family," Tam yells out the open door.

"Zebb?" I stare up at him.

"You said you took vacations to ignore the holiday, but they weren't family trips. Let's make new memories for you."

"You want me to travel with you?" I glance around him and find Tam smiling big from where she dangles over something, to hang her head before the open door. "This is crazy."

"No crazier than letting you go when we were young. Now I have you back and I don't want a day to pass without you. Let's see where this goes. You and me. Us on a bus."

"That's such a Dad rhyme."

"I am a dad but I'm also a man, wanting the woman before him to be his." Zebb reaches for my hands and squeezes.

"I am yours, Zebb. I always have been." We stare at one another, eyes caught and smiles spreading.

"Give me this. Time together. This can be your Christmas gift to me." Zebb's voice is quiet as he swipes his thumb over my knuckles.

Time. It can't be produced, bought, or sold. It doesn't come in a box with ribbons and bows. It comes from the heart and given without cost.

"I can do that," I whisper.

"Then get packing. The road awaits." He releases my hands, spins me toward my building and smacks my backside.

Tam giggles.

"Where are we going? What should I pack?" Excitement fills me. I'm going in a real RV, on a real vacation, like a real family.

"A little bit of everything," Zebb says, and I still don't know what that means.

"And look, Eva. I brought you some new angel wings." Tam awkwardly holds out a new set of wings that are much smaller than the ones I'd given her, but still just as wonderful. "Daddy says we're going to fly down the highway."

"Thanks Tam." I'd cry but I can't seem to stop smiling.

"Go," Zebb whispers, leaning forward and giving me a quick kiss. He walks backward two steps. "Oh, and bring that serendipity mitten. Fate might need it."

Because we're a pair.

He winks and then turns toward the RV.

I rush upstairs and toss a collection of I don't even know what into a bag, including a new lingerie piece I was saving for Valentine's Day. As one holiday ends, another begins so to speak.

Once I'm back downstairs and climbing into the passenger seat beside Zebb, I laugh. "Can you drive this thing?"

"I drive fire engines. I can handle this rig."

I turn back to Tam, who's buckling a seatbelt at the mini-kitchen table.

"Hey, Tam. I'm going to kiss your dad, so don't look."

"Ugh." She rolls her eyes and crosses her arms on the table. Then lowers her head to shield her sight. "I'm counting to ten."

I lean toward Zebb and he meets me half way.

"Ten, nine . . ."

I don't hear the rest of her numbers. When the countdown ends, it won't matter. I'll be kissing this man more and more in the future.

Where we'll be on a new adventure, together.

epilogue

One year later

"Hello, and welcome to Gingersnaps." I greet customers as they enter. My specialty shop is not located downtown but in a smaller neighborhood within Chicago. We also have a strong online presence, but I love when people come into the store. We've made a reputation for ourselves with our novelty gift items.

And as we're about to celebrate our first Christmas, for the first time since I can remember, I'm excited for the holiday to happen.

However, the most important part of this holiday is what I learned last year.

The gift of time is the most precious present.

Zebb, Tam, and I spent ten days on the road in the rented RV where we learned more about each other. And the learning didn't end when we returned to Chicago. Zebb didn't leave me behind.

Tonight, on the eve of Christmas, I'll celebrate with Zebb and Tam. Tomorrow after Santa makes a visit, which might be Zebb's final chance to pretend the big man is real with Tam, we'll join the rest of his family at his mother's place.

Marnie and Lisa will be there with their new baby boy.

Brock will be present with Nick and Eleanor.

And Zebb's mother will welcome me as she's done from the start.

I'm part of the family.

The ring on my finger binds me to them even more.

Zebb and I had a small family affair wedding in June under a canopy at the park near Lake Michigan. Then we went to our backyard for a catered meal. We didn't have a maid of honor or a best man. We had Tam stand up for both of us.

Zebb gave me the ultimate wedding present: him.

+ + +

When the day finally ends—we close promptly at six every evening—I head home to Zebb and Tam who are making dinner. Every corner of the house drips with holiday decorations and cheer. Love fills this home, making the holidays all that more special.

Later, Tam is nestled in bed, and Zebb and I are alone in our room, and this is the moment I've anticipated all day.

"I bought a present for my husband," I begin, calling from our bathroom. "And I think he should open it tonight."

"Your husband, huh?" A cocky grin fills his voice, acknowledging that he likes the label.

I round the bathroom entrance. "Have you been a good man this year?"

Zebb is sitting on the edge of our bed, his jaw dropping. He swallows as his eyes roam up my body, then he's vigorously shaking his head. "Nope. Naughty. Very naughty."

I'm wearing the sexy Santa outfit from last year with one little addition. I approach Zebb and stand before him, swiping my hands through his hair as his fingers coast up my thighs, teasing me until his hands flatten and his palms skim under the sheer panels. His hand catches on something and he pauses.

"What's this?" He pulls back one side of the lingerie and notices the red ribbon tied around my waist.

"Unwrap me," I whisper, still combing through his hair. Zebb pulls the ribbon, and the bow comes undone. He leans forward and kisses me near my belly button.

"Merry Christmas to me," he softly chuckles, thinking I'm the present.

And I am, but so is something else.

I lower my hand to my belly and cup his scruff-covered jaw with my other hand. Gently prodding him to look up at me, I tip my chin to imply my stomach.

"Merry Christmas, Zebb."

He stares at me, then glances down at my hand over my stomach. "Is this . . ." He looks up at me.

"A Christmas miracle."

Zebb stares up at me, eyes softening. We'd talked about his guilt over losing Mary and his fear it could happen again. We hadn't planned to have any children other than Tam. She's a handful in a good way.

But stranger things have happened.

"I'm pregnant." Suddenly, I'm worried Zebb won't be as happy as I am. I took a test a week ago and confirmed the results with a doctor two days ago. Holding in this secret has been almost impossible, but I wanted to be certain. I wanted to give him the only physical present I could think of to give him.

Zebb leans forward and kisses my belly again. Then he wraps his arms around me and tugs me to him, laying his cheek on my stomach. I continue to comb through his hair, loving this man.

"This is the best gift. Thank you."

Cupping his jaw, I tug his face, so he looks up at me. "You're the best gift."

Zebb shakes his head, and softly chuckles. "I'm going to appreciate the fuck out of you."

Then, he's dragging me over him on our bed and we unwrap the rest of our gift to one another.

Our love.

Thank you for taking the time to read SCROOGE-ish.

Please consider writing a review on major sales channels where ebooks and paperbacks are sold and discussed.
Next up in the HOLIDAY HOTTIES: NAUGHTY-ish.
A naughty, next-door neighbor, holiday romance.

When a single mom struggles to find the fa-la-la in the holiday season, her naughty next-door neighbor decides to bring her a little comfort and joy to restore her faith in the magic of the most wonderful time of the year (and love).

Turn the page for a sample.

Naughty-ish

If you like firefighter romances, you might also enjoy
THE SEX EDUCATION OF M.E.
When a widowed professor decides dating is back in the books, her new neighbor - a silver fox fireman - volunteers to school her in rekindling a flame between the sheets.

OR TRY

STERLING BRICK
When high school lovers reunite twenty-years later while locked in the men's bathroom during a funeral, this silver fox fireman is set on reigniting their old flame.

Author Note

Like Eva, I'm really not a fan of Christmas anymore. The commercialism over the years has robbed it of its luster. Christmas has almost become a competition. Who can give a better gift? But that isn't the meaning behind this holiday in the Christian world, and each year, I have to force myself to remember Dr. Seuss's famous words: *"Maybe Christmas, he thought, doesn't come from a store. Maybe Christmas, perhaps, means a little bit more."*

I live in Chicago. While Mr. Dunbar and I didn't grow up here (having moved here in our early twenties), we have raised our children on the edge of the city. One of our holiday traditions was eating dinner or having breakfast with Santa at the iconic Marshall Field's department store on State Street downtown. Unfortunately, Field's was eventually acquired and sold, and then acquired once more, and became a Macy's Department Store. Now I have nothing against Macy's, but Macy's says New York. I really wish Chicago could have kept just one Marshall Field's location, making it an original experience, like shopping at Liberty London in London.

But no one asked me.

Because I have a vivid imagination, and I write fiction, I've written my dream. Ashford's is the landmark flagship store on State Street, and The Tea Room is based off the Walnut Room on the sixth floor of the original Marshall Fields.

Another tradition that began as my girls grew older was a visit to American Girl Place, originally on Chicago Avenue. Their birthday teas, after-school teas, and Christmas concert and tea were a little girl's dream (and maybe a big mama's dream as well). I've taken the liberty to combine some favorite events into one experience.

Finally, I want to give a shout out to Charles Dickens. *A Christmas Carol* isn't necessarily one of my favorite Christmas tales. (I'm partial to *The Family Stone* which is a whole other story.) But as a former

English teacher, and someone who has studied Dickens' play in numerous ways, this story of transformation is classic.

A visit into the past. A new perspective of the present. A glimpse of the future.

Nothing causes change better than reflection.

So if you're reading this during the holiday season, I hope you experience comforting confession and peace with yourself. Any change you want to see, really starts with self-examination and willingness to transform.

Be true to yourself. Be kind to others.

Embrace love.

Happy holidays.

<u>Naughty-ish</u>

1

Where is that fucking elf on a shelf doll?

In preparation for the upcoming Christmas holiday, I'd been searching everywhere for that damn creepy imp that sits on a shelf, pretending to monitor my children's behavior in the weeks before the holiday.

Naughty or nice, Nash and Eloise are my favorite two people in the world.

But that elf really annoys me.

I couldn't keep the festive doll with the other decorations for fear the kids would discover him, thus ruining the ploy that he appears on the Feast of St. Nicholas. A tradition which includes setting out your shoes—in our case, by the front door—and if you are on Santa's nice list, candy fills your footwear. A kid on the naughty list receives a lump of coal.

My parents used this setup when I was a child, which was long before that shelf elf was even imagined. It was another gimmick propagated by adults to keep their children in line during the holiday season.

"If you're on the naughty list, there's still time to right wrongs."

I've said those very words myself, although my children are not bad kids. They aren't angels by any stretch, but with the year we've had, they're damn near perfect. My ex-husband is the one who belongs on the naughty list. Actually, he belongs on the dirtbag's list, but that's neither here nor there tonight as I tackle my first holiday season without his presence. I want it to be a pleasant Christmas for my little ones. They deserve it.

"Shoes," I mutter aloud, standing in the wintery darkness of ten o'clock in my living room.

Before the kids went to bed, Nash put his gym shoes by the front door beside Eloise's Sherpa-lined boots. She thought St. Nick might bring her more candy if she had taller footwear. *St. Nick is on a budget this year, kiddo.* Of course, she doesn't know the tradition is all make-believe. There isn't a saint named Nick checking in on us. There isn't even a Santa Claus, but I'll wait a few years before breaking her heart on that one.

Lord knows she'll have bigger heartbreaks in her life. I'll shield her as best I can, for as long as I can. But what happens when she's older and on her own? What do I do if she ends up like me, marrying a schmuck?

Mitch hadn't been a schmuck when we married. He was everything I'd been looking for in my early thirties. What does the heart know though, right? Good sex brought us together, but it apparently wasn't good enough because he eventually went elsewhere.

Once. It only happened once.

On a scale of zero times it should have happened, his infidelity occurred one time too many.

His decision shattered me. No marriage is perfect, but that kind of slip-up means there was an issue I hadn't noticed buried underneath the daily life of a married couple with young children. I faulted myself in some ways. Not for him stepping out on me. That was all on him. However, I'd been blinded by a sense of security I had with my ex-husband. And blindsided by his actions.

Now I was forty, wiser, and wary.

And Mitch's construction boots are conspicuously absent from our collection this year.

"Shoes," I mumble again. Snapping my fingers, I recall what I was doing—looking for the elf. Eventually, he'll be placed on top of the fridge or the china cabinet because he needs to be out of reach from Nash, who is only five. At eight years old, Eloise is the one with questions. And shoes are the answer tonight, as the wily elf is in a shoebox on a shelf in my closet—a place the children would never go.

Climbing the stairs of my new-to-us home, I find the little rascal in an old box for heels I no longer own. Once retrieved, I look about the house seeking a good spot to place him. Eloise already wrote him a long list of questions, and I'll need to forage through her letters from last year (also placed in the box) to recall previous answers. She's a smart one, my little girl, and she remembers this shit better than me.

As the litany of her questions spans a sheet of paper front and back, a glass of wine is in order to navigate this process. As a right-handed person, I'll have to disguise my handwriting by using my left hand to write the answers. A full glass of red matches the holiday spirit, I decide, although I don't have a stitch of decoration up in this house yet. I haven't had time. Returning to full-time work after the divorce, plus carpools for extracurricular activities, and the daily grind of getting my children to and from school, then dinner and homework, baths and bedtime routines, I'm beat by the end of the day.

Besides, Thanksgiving was just over a week ago.

After a hardy drink, I focus on the first question.

Number one. Do you like peppermint dick?

I blink, certain I've misread and realize I have.

Do you like peppermint stick?

Sweet baby Jesus in a manger, my imagination got the best of me there, or perhaps it's more my subconscious, as I haven't been with a man in over a year. Feeling dirty and unwanted after what Mitch did, the dry spell hadn't bothered me at first, but now, twelve months later, I miss the sensual touch of another human. My own fingers have worked willingly but not provided the wonder of connecting with someone else.

Number two. How many—

THUNK!

"What the hell?" I glance over my shoulder, peering behind me through the small window in the eating area. Something has just hit my house.

Another thud and then something clatters outside, out of sight of the window.

"When up on the rooftop, there arose such a clatter," I mutter the famous line from Clement Clarke Moore's poem *'Twas the Night Before Christmas*."

Standing, I hold my breath, awaiting another thump when a different thought wafts through my head. The poem is actually titled *A Visit from St. Nick*.

Impossible.

Bemused, I breathily laugh at myself. Clearly, I need more sleep.

Willing my shoulders to relax, I prepare to sit back down when I hear the telltale sign of an aluminum ladder clanking and a light thud of metal connecting with my house again.

On second thought, is the verse *arose such a ladder?*

Shaking my head, I realize I'm losing my mind, but something is definitely banging on the side of my home. With wineglass in hand as if that will protect me, I slip into my own set of Sherpa-lined boots and step out the back door leading to the driveway I share with my neighbor. My single car garage is detached from the house, and I don't park in the slightly leaning building. The space covers bikes, summer furniture, and boxes I haven't unpacked yet. We've only been in the house for seven months.

Standing on the back stoop, I pause. *What am I doing?* I'm a single mother living alone. I shouldn't be out here investigating in the dark.

Then I hear the metal clang of a ladder against the siding once more coming from my front yard and curiosity gets the best of me. Despite the cold, I walk along the side of my home and down the drive toward the front. Cupping the wineglass against my chest, I slowly approach the corner of my house.

"Shit." A deep male voice whispers in the night.

My heartbeat ratchets up a few thumps. *Is someone trying to break in?* They're making quite a racket if that's the case. Not to mention, the only thing of value in this house are my two children *nestled all snug in their beds*.

Rounding the corner, I shout, "What the hell are you doing?"

My sharp voice rips through the quiet night air, causing the man standing on the low roof overhanging my front stoop to slip. With a curse from his lips and the slide of his feet, he scrambles to stay on the narrow strip of roofing. Only his left foot goes over the edge, kicking the gutter.

He does an awkward split motion before his body slowly glides to the end of the roof, and his weight takes him off it.

"Oh my God!" I cry out, rushing toward the large body dangling from the overhang. Not more than ten feet from the ground to the start of the incline, his stretched form shows he's roughly six feet plus. He only has a few feet to drop if he lets go of my gutter, which is starting to strain under his weight. He's too far away to reach the ladder, which is propped up on the opposite corner of the overhang. With a swing of long legs in jeans that accentuate the thickness of his thighs and the firmness of his backside, he tucks forward before lunging back and dropping like a cat to the ground, clearing the stairs that descend from the porch. His back remains to me for half a second, and red buffalo check flannel strains over the expanse of thick muscles and flexed biceps in a shirt that hugs his body. Slowly, he turns to face me.

"Nick?" I choke.

With a bright red knit cap on his head, my next-door neighbor stares down at me. He has these intense, dark blue eyes and cheeks like cliffs, matching the mountainous stature of his body. His jaw holds an artful combination of black and white scruff, which is more snow than earth-colored despite his hair still being a shade of charcoal.

And I know these details about Nick, my next-door neighbor, because he's hot with a capital H.

Nick Santos was already living next door when the kids and I moved in. My first interaction with him was when I'd pulled into my driveway one evening to find him making out with a woman against his front door. He didn't break away from her mouth until I'd parked my car, gotten out, and walked toward my front entrance. Only a sliver of grass separates our single car driveways.

I hadn't wanted to look at them, but it was hard to pull away from the sight of his body pressing some woman against the building. His thick leg between her thighs. His hands on her sides. Her arms were around his neck, hands in his hair. He was going for a breast when he pulled back from her and turned his head toward me. Our eyes locked and his gleamed in the early darkness.

Then, like a frightened mouse, I'd scampered toward my house with my head down.

The next time I'd seen him was a week or so later. Shouts and curses came from the house next door. I had been leaving for work sans children, thankfully, as the display in his yard included him standing on the lawn and the woman who I assumed was the one from the week before tossing items out the front door, calling him names I'd never heard and stringing together profanity that might make a sailor blush.

Nick had stood stoic and firm with his legs spread wide, arms crossed, one hand lifted to his chin, slowly stroking thick fingers over that beautiful layering of ink and chrome hair on his jaw.

Hours later, he'd ripped out of his driveway on his motorcycle.

Questions had flitted through my mind at the time. Was she the same woman or someone different? Had he cheated on her or were they the same hot-for-each-other couple from one week ago? The scene had been a reminder of how quickly a relationship can flip. And for some reason I felt sorry for him.

Another week had passed before I'd seen him again, tinkering under the hood of a large pickup truck in his portion of the shared driveway. On that day, I'd been returning from work. Walking up my side of the drive, something prompted me to stop and address him despite us never having exchanged a word previously.

"Are you okay?"

He'd tipped his head. Surprise had been evident in his hard expression before he stood straighter and turned his face in the direction of his front yard.

"Nothing that hasn't happened before," he'd huffed and leaned forward, half-hidden underneath the hood again. "Might have been more effective if it wasn't my house, though."

Puzzled by his explanation, I didn't move from my spot. "Well, I just wanted to make certain you were all right."

He didn't respond at first, but his body stilled once more.

"*I'm Holliday,*" *I'd offered.* "*That's with two l's.*" *There's irony in the name, and I'd waited for him to comment, but he didn't.* "*My children are Eloise and Nash.*"

I'd paused, thinking he would introduce himself. Or not.

"*Just thought you should know.*" *I'd previously lived in a neighborhood where everyone knew each other's names and the names of their children. It takes a village. Then again, that village knew everyone else's business.*

Like how my ex-husband cheated on me while attending a reunion at his alma mater. A rambunctious Big Ten football game led to post-game shenanigans with his college sweetheart.

This new-to-me neighborhood, however, consisted of mainly older homes with elderly residents, and I was out of my element here.

With the growing silence between my neighbor and me, I'd turned on my heels and headed toward my back door.

"*I'm Nick,*" *he'd finally stated.*

I'd stopped walking but hadn't spun to face him before he added, "*You should get your old man to cut the grass.*"

Glancing at what I could see of my yard, I'd taken offense at several things.

One, I didn't have an old man.

Two, I was aware my grass was overgrown, but I didn't have a mower yet—it was just one more item on a list of growing necessities.

And three, I could take care of my own damn lawn, even if I wasn't certain that was true. I didn't need an old man *to do it for me.*

"*I'll get right on that,*" *I'd muttered, turning only my head over my shoulder and giving him a friendly salute when what I really wanted to do was give him the finger.* "*Nice to meet you.*" *Sarcasm had dripped in my tone. So much for being neighborly.*

However, within a few days, the drone of a lawnmower filled the air, and the sound came particularly close to my home. When I'd stepped out on my front stoop, Nick was mowing my grass.

"*What the hell are you doing?*" *I'd snapped, wondering what he was playing at by encroaching on my yard. I'd said I'd take care of it.*

But I didn't have a viable plan. I'd considered asking Mitch if I could borrow his lawnmower, the one I'd bought him two years ago as a Father's Day present, but the thought of asking Mitch for anything made me sick.

The loud hum of the mower cut off, and Nick halted in my yard. Looking up at me, he clutched the handle of his mower.

"I wanted to apologize." Those dark eyes were sparkling sapphires under the bright summer sunshine. "Your kid told me you're . . ."

The unspoken word could be one of many.

Single? Divorced? Helpless?

"I'll speak to my children about bothering the neighbors." I crossed my arms and stared back at him.

His arms were covered in tattoos, and some even crept up his neck, sticking out from the collar of his tee, which was plastered to his chest from the exertion. A giant wet stain formed between the solid flat of his pecs beneath the cotton. Jeans covered his legs, accenting the curve of firm thigh muscles. He wore a baseball cap on his head. He was a beautiful man—slightly dangerous-looking but gorgeous nonetheless—and he was sweet to cut my grass, even if it was out of pity.

"I can pay you," I'd stated.

He'd tipped up a brow. "Consider it my apology."

"For what?" Kissing a woman on his front porch? Fighting with said woman in his yard? Or insulting me about needing a man to tend my lawn?

"I can take care of it." I'd nodded at the grass. I didn't need his apology. I was only being friendly that day when I'd asked about his well-being, foolishly thinking we were kindred spirits through our relationship failures. I had been wrong. He didn't need to prove anything to me.

Heading into the house for my last twenty-dollar bill, I'd returned to find the mower running again. Walking up to him, I held out the money. He'd stilled but didn't cut off the mower this time. He'd stared at the bill in my hand.

"Don't want it!" he'd hollered over the drone of the lawn mower.

"I'd feel better if you take it." My pride was on the line. I'd flicked my wrist once, emphasizing the outstretched twenty.

His gaze lifted, and those sharp eyes met mine. "Buy yourself something pretty with it, and we'll call us even."

Oh, he was smooth. But I wasn't having that nonsense.

I'd folded the bill in my hand and pursed my lips, knowing my next move was bold. I stepped back, allowing him to step forward. Then as he passed me, I slipped the twenty into his back pocket, getting an unintentional swipe of the firmness of one globe, stretching worn denim over his ass.

He'd stopped abruptly, twisting his upper body and staring down at my retreating hand.

"Buy yourself something pretty," I'd taunted and stomped away from him. I wasn't going to owe him, neighbor or not.

That was back in June.

In the cold of December, the night air is seeping through my thin, long-sleeved shirt and pajama shorts. What was I thinking stepping out here wearing boots and wielding a wineglass?

"Where's your jacket?" Nick snipes, stepping toward me, hands reaching forward to rub up and down my arms. I'd pulled them in close, huddling them against my chest as I hopped from foot to foot, waiting for him to explain what he'd been doing on my roof.

However, the freezing chill skittering over my skin disappears under the warmth of his calloused palms. His proximity infuses my entire body with a rush of heat, that ignites something in the depths of my cold bones. The faint scent of bayberry and snow tickles my nose, awakening all my senses. Forget my wine, I'm intoxicated by his nearness.

"I heard a noise," I stammer, struggling to remember what he asked me.

"Sorry about that." He removes his hands, and instantly, I miss the heat of his touch.

He tips his head, sheepishly peering down at the ground.

"What are you doing out here?" I nod at my roof, noting the ladder and some tools plus a cardboard box, resting on the shingles.

"I was hanging Christmas lights."

"On *my* house?"

"You're bringing down the block," he teases as he'd done the remainder of the summer when I still hadn't purchased a lawnmower.

My dad eventually bought me a mower from a garage sale in September, but as I struggled to start the thing, Nick appeared and told me he'd upkeep the lawn as he had most of the previous months. He continued to refuse my money.

"I hadn't gotten to it." The phrase was becoming the story of my life.

For the sake of my children, my intentions for the holiday season were well-meaning, but I haven't decorated yet. I haven't purchased any gifts. I haven't planned any seasonal activities. As a single mom, working full-time, I was doing the best I could living on a budget of time and finances. Which roughly translated to, I didn't have the *ho-ho-ho* energy I've had in years' past.

My Christmas spirit was waning this year, like that one pesky bulb causing an entire strand of lights to go out.

However, as Nick looks at me, his eyes twinkle like the little blue lights I've seen in other people's yards. And a teeny-tiny spark inside me wants to do better. Be better.

"What are *you* doing out here? It's freezing." His hands return to my arms, rubbing up and down once again. Immediately, the warmth melts over my skin, heating me up like a cozy winter fire.

"I thought you were the sugar plum fairy breaking in."

Nick laughs, hearty and full, rich like the wine in my glass.

"You don't need to do this," I remind him, repeating what I'd said dozens of times to him over the past few months. He feels sorry for me. That's why he does what he does. I'm that single mother neighbor who will one day let cats overrun her home when her children grow older and leave her alone, forgetting she exists.

The thought is pathetic and sobering.

"I want to," he states, as he's said often enough.

"Nash and Eloise will love it," I say, hoping my children's happiness means something to him. He's friendly with them. He even played catch with Nash a few times this fall when Mitch didn't show up for his scheduled weeknight visits. Nick also praised Eloise's chalk drawings, allowing her to overtake his driveway when ours is full of sketches.

"I want *you* to love it," he says, his eyes still on me.

I'd offer to pay him for the lights or his time, but I already know he'll reject the gesture. After my bold move last summer to slip a twenty in his pocket, I've never attempted to touch him again. I've made him cookies and casseroles, bought pots with flowers for his porch, and left him a case of beer on occasion. I didn't know how else to repay him for his kindness.

"It will look beautiful." I'm not really certain how it will look, but the roofline was made for Christmas lights. If he edges the front porch overhang and wraps lights over the dormers on the taller roof like he did his own home, the twinkling magic will bring cheer to my little house.

I like the place with its three small bedrooms on the second floor and its subtle front stoop raised up a few steps as typical Chicago homes are. Our previous home in the suburbs was double the size with manicured landscaping and a koi pond. Still, this place is mine and I smile in spite of myself.

"Thank you." My voice is quiet as my teeth chatter.

"Get inside." He winks with a tilt of his head toward the front door. "I'll try not to make too much noise."

"Try not to fall off the roof," I warn with a laugh in my throat.

"You startled me." His eyes narrow a bit, focusing on my face until his gaze drifts to the pebbled nipples poking out beneath my thin sleep shirt. He doesn't take his gaze from my chest.

I breathily answer him. "You surprised me."

His Adam's apple bobs, and he pulls his head upward, turning to give me the side of his face. "Go inside, Holliday." His deep voice roughens, and his jaw clenches.

The strangest sensation washes over me. I want to kiss up the column of his throat, outline the edge of his jaw with my lips, and climb his body like the evergreen he is.

The thought isn't entirely offhand as I've had several similar fantasies throughout the summer and into fall about him. I'm highly attracted to my neighbor, though it's ridiculous to feel this way.

"You're going to catch a cold," he adds, breaking into my vision of slipping my arms inside his red-checked flannel and pressing my cool tits to his warm chest.

His words are a reminder he isn't attracted to me.

He just feels sorry for the single mom next door.

Continue reading <u>NAUGHTY-ish</u>.

Naughty-ish

More by L.B. Dunbar

Sterling Falls
Seven small-town siblings muddle their way through love over 40.
Sterling Heat
Sterling Brick
Sterling Streak
Sterling Clay
Sterling Fight
Sterling Touch
Sterling Stone

Chicago Anchors
When your eyes are on the silver fox coach, more than the ball.
Elevator Pitch
Catch the Kiss

Parentmoon
When the mother of the groom goes head-to-head with the single father
of the bride.

Holiday Hotties (Christmas novellas)
Holiday novellas certain to heat the season.
Scrooge-ish
Naughty-ish
Grouch-ish

Road Trips & Romance
Three sisters. Three destinations. All second chances at love over 40.
Hauling Ashe
Merging Wright
Rhode Trip

Lakeside Cottage
Four friends. Four summers. Shenanigans and love happen at the lake.
Living at 40
Loving at 40
Learning at 40
Letting Go at 40

L.B. DUNBAR

The Silver Foxes of Blue Ridge
Small mountain town, silver foxes. Brothers seeking love over 40.
Silver Brewer
Silver Player
Silver Mayor
Silver Biker

Sexy Silver Foxes
When sexy silver foxes meet the feisty vixens of their dreams.
After Care
Midlife Crisis
Restored Dreams
Second Chance
Wine&Dine

Collision novellas
A spin-off from After Care – the younger set/rock stars
Collide
Caught

The Sex Education of M.E.
The original sexy silver fox.
When a widowed professor decides she'd like to date again, and a local
fireman volunteers to give her lessons.

The Heart Collection
Small town, big hearts - stories of family and love.
Speak from the Heart
Read with your Heart
Look with your Heart
Fight from the Heart
View with your Heart

A Heart Collection Spin-off
The Heart Remembers

BOOKS IN OTHER AUTHOR WORLDS

<u>Smartypants Romance (an imprint of Penny Reid)</u>
Tales of the Winters sisters set in Green Valley.
Love in Due Time
Love in Deed
Love in a Pickle

<u>The World of True North (an imprint of Sarina Bowen)</u>
Welcome to Vermont! And the Busy Bean Café.
Cowboy
Studfinder

THE EARLY YEARS
<u>The Legendary Rock Star Series</u>
A classic tale with a modern twist of rockstar romance and suspense.

<u>Paradise Stories</u>
MMA romance. Two brothers. One fight.

<u>The Island Duet</u>
Intrigue and suspense. The island knows what you've done.

<u>Modern Descendants – writing as elda lore</u>
Magical realism. Modern myths of Greek gods.

About the Author

www.lbdunbar.com

L.B. Dunbar loves sexy silver foxes, second chances, and small towns. If you enjoy older characters in your romance reads, including a hero with a little silver in his scruff and a heroine rediscovering her worth, then welcome to romance for those over 40. L.B. Dunbar's signature works include women and men in their prime taking another turn at love and happily ever after. She's a *USA TODAY* Bestseller as well as #1 Bestseller on Amazon in Later in Life Romance with her Lakeside Cottage and Road Trips & Romance series. L.B. lives in Chicago with her own sexy silver fox.

To get all the scoop about the self-proclaimed queen of silver fox romance, join her on Facebook at Loving L.B. or receive her monthly newsletter, Love Notes.

+++

Connect with L.B. Dunbar